CONVERSION
PARTY

ANTHONY S. BUONI

CONVERSION PARTY, second edition

Transmunande Press, LLC | www.transmundanepress.com
Editor-in-Chief & Co-Publisher: Alisha Chambers
Content Editor & Co-Publisher: Anthony S. Buoni
Conversion Party is copyright © 2012 by Anthony S. Buoni
through Transmundane Press, LLC. All rights reserved.

Cover Design: Adam Ake
Interior Layout: Alisha Chambers

ISBN-13: 978-0-9984983-6-2

Worldwide Rights
Created in the United States of America

DEDICATION

This book is dedicated to all the starfighters, past, present, and future.
Stay gold, cats.
.

Horror, in literature and film, constantly mutates. What frightened those brave enough to wander toward eldritch tales and cinema house spook shows yesterday often does not provide substantial fear for readers and viewers today. Death and mayhem splattered across newspapers and flat screens has desensitized audiences, and this unflinching, globalized bombardment of terrors has forced authors and filmmakers to up the ante in order to keep the scares fresh and fans scared, a progression that has both helped and hurt the genre.

Longtime book and movie darlings, Vampires never wane in popularity. From DRACULA, Bram Stoker's titular bloodsucker has been rehashed numerous times on the silver screen. Early incarnations such as Max Schreck's frightening Nosferatu and Bela Lugosi's elegant Count Dracula delivered tension through subtle performances, fog-swept gothic castles, and grainy black and white cinematography. Such romantic entities have shifted into the savage beings in 30 DAYS of NIGHT and the oversexed TRUE BLOOD vamps of Charlaine Harris lore. Despite such monstrous leeches, modern vampires have taken a simultaneous step back. Undead Edward Cullen is a gentleman way past his promise ring marriage to the vestal Bella in the teen-geared TWILIGHT franchise. Legions of similar books aimed at intermediate readers have corrupted the vampire's essence; overblowing these once mysterious and frightening creatures into violent, pornographic, sparkling caricatures.

Ghosts have also moved from mystic realms into blasé mediocrity. In past, establishments purported haunted were shunned and avoided at all costs. What sane soul would spend the night within such accursed edifices? Greek myth sent lovelorn Orpheus into the feared Underworld after Eurydice, and Victorian yarns such as Edward Bulwer-Lytton's THE HAUNTED AND THE HAUNTERS matched a stoic adventurer against a phantasmal flat in a test of wills. Literary apparitions crossed media territories, dazzling moviegoers with double-exposed footage in Swedish director Victor Sjöström's THE PHANTOM CARRIAGE. Such restrained, cutting-edge specters are now near-forgotten, replaced by CG wraiths leaping from viral videotapes and threatening to poison every friend in your social network. Worse, most cable channels offer prime time programs centered on educated minds running down disembodied apparitions with high-tech gadgetry viewers can purchase at online novelty shops. Though belief in ghosts is currently stronger than ever, people now visit places formerly dodged in hopes of rubbing shoulders with death.

As the world cowered from all-too-real nuclear threats in the 1950s and '60s, a new fiend emerged from the mushroom cloud shadows. When Michael Powell's PEEPING TOM and Alfred Hitchcock's PSYCHO were released, monsters—no longer confined to supernatural spheres and B movies—became the smiling, awkward stranger flirting with you over tea, and serial killers took their place forever in horror's pantheon. Embodying something sinister lurking in us all, mass murderers were a sign of the times. Newspapers and television reported more and more on communities rattled by heinous crimes, and books and cinema raced to out shock previous jaunts into entertainment's dark side. The material became gorier, paving the way for vicious slasher film franchises (such as HALLOWEEN, FRIDAY the 13th, and A NIGHTMARE on ELM STREET) where audiences cheered on killers instead of fearing them. Recent films such as Eli Roth's HOSTEL and the continuing SAW franchise have taken slice-and-dice violence to the next level, spending time and energy on gross-out effects at the price of anticipation and plot.

Evolutionary strides aside, no matter how shocking or lurid these books and films become, at their hearts they remain morality stories. Characters engaging in less-than-honorable behavior often meet disturbing ends while those virtuous are usually spared.

From Victorian vampires seducing women with a wanton, hypnotizing gaze and sipping blood from the necks of sleeping virgins to serial killers using phallic symbols such as knives to stab showering, vulnerable women, sex has always been one of the core elements of horror. Stories of bloodsucking concubines seducing the chaste, nosferatu feeding off prostitutes, and undead eternal love pepper vampire tradition. Ghosts haunt in the name of unrequited love, loom in the areas they were violated of their human existences, and lure lonely souls to their doom. In any slasher film, the fastest way to go toes up is to fool around, especially in premarital relations. PSYCHO's catalyst occurs thirty minutes in when an adulterous thief on the lam finds her gruesome fate in the very place she sought refuge. On the flipside, when chaste characters (usually women dubbed "survivor girls") do not participate in hanky-panky, drug use, or other illicit activities, they stand up for morals and subsequently against the pursuing monsters, coming out saving the day, the last one left alive, and making the message clear: bad deeds are punished and good actions are rewarded.

Although the genre's archetypes run deep, human desire to be shocked runs deeper. When a story or film outshines reality in its wickedness, the return from the fictional abyss makes the world seem less evil. Horror is a coping mechanism for real life's woes, allowing it to morph to suit the needs of current events, no matter how repulsive it may seem.

CONVERSION PARTY blends these horror tropes. The main character, Doug, is a combination of literature and cinematic monsters. He is a vampire in the sense that he is a creature of the night, feeding off friends, people also living on the fringe. Doug's desire to catch and distribute STDs is reminiscent of spreading vampirism or a zombie plague, health and vitality giving way to malady and death. Passing through life barely tangible and haunting clubs, he is a ghost, not alive but not exactly dead. Finally, he is a serial killer. Not in the form of a stranger emerging from the shadows, but as that smiling friend you've invited into the most intimate aspects of your life. Sharing bed and body with him, you find that within this confidence you've been debased. However, instead of attacking with some phallic symbol, Doug is actually using his penis to rip your life apart, turning trust into the ultimate weapon.

Gory with its lascivious subject matter, CONVERSION PARTY explores the dark side of counter culture. Its screenplay format links that spectral veil between literature and film, a place CONVERSION PARTY feels like home, no matter how haunted that house may be. Despite unfolding inside a world with blurred lines of good and evil, moral lessons creep across the page like grave frost; yet it is up to you, the reader, to decide who the monsters are.

Anthony S. Buoni
25 December 2011 / 6 August 2017
Panama City Beach, Fl / New Orleans, LA

ACKNOWLEDGMENTS

Special thanks to **LYNN WALLACE**, for teaching us all and for the screenplay class this tale originated; **AARON BEARDEN** for cheering this project on over the past decade; **JOHN RAMOS** and **JOEY FILIP** for listening to it develop over many cold beers as I wrote on the clock; **CONRAD YOUNG** for running lines with me so I could hear the dialog; **Tony Viejo II, Brittany M. Lamoureux, Kim Renfroe, Anthony Englehardt, Rob Blanchette** and **Michele Skelly-Bland** for early faith in the story and spreading the myth of it; **Adelle Davis** for pushing me to finish what I started; **Michael Lister** for warm, open arms and loving guidance. Also, **Mom**, **Dad**, and **Fallon** for living with a haunted writer.
Without you cats, this would not exist.

FADE IN:

INT. LIVING ROOM—LATE AFTERNOON

A TV flickers in a cozy living room, illuminating green leather couches, a nice stereo, and a coffee table.

DOUG, late-twenties, blue eyes, dark hair, and dressed in a heavy metal T-shirt and torn blue jeans, paces in front of the TV while fighting with his girlfriend, SAM.

Sam—27-years-old, large hoop earrings, and a small, diamond nose ring—fidgets with the straps on a yellow sundress,

                    SAM

          I saw you kissing her,
          asshole. No bullshit
          excuses this time—I caught
          you in the act.

                    DOUG

          I couldn't help it, she was
          beautiful.

                    SAM

          Just because someone is
          pretty doesn't mean you
          have to kiss or fuck her.

                    DOUG

I love *you*, Sam.

                    SAM

But you'll screw anything
with a pulse.

                    DOUG

A pulse is optional.

                    SAM

That's sick. What if you
catch something on one of
your sexual escapades? I
know you, and you're not
always safe.

                    DOUG

I guess I'll just have to
deal with it.

                    SAM

You and me both. Whatever
you catch you'll bring home
to me. There is a lot of
nasty shit out there, and I
don't want it—not even if
it comes from you.

DOUG

Does this mean we're
breaking up?

SAM

Goddamn right it does. I'm
not gonna stand by and wait
for you to give me AIDS.

DOUG

But, honey, that was the
plan all along.

SAM

What?

DOUG

You don't think that
sharing HIV would be
erotic?

SAM

EROTIC? Are you fucking
delirious?

DOUG

No. It's a total turn on.
It heightens the sensuality
of sex.

SAM

You're talking nonsense.
HIV is a terrible plague.

DOUG

It's sexy.

Sam stammers as Doug pulls a Camel
cigarette out of a silver cigarette
case. He puts the smoke to his lips
and sparks a Zippo lighter. Before he
gets the flame to the end of the
cigarette, Sam spits in his face.

SAM

You fucking suck. Don't
call me tonight or ever,
Doug.

Sam EXITS the house, slamming the door
on her way out. A framed picture of
Bob Dylan falls to the floor, cracking
the glass.

DOUG

Go to hell, bitch.

Doug wipes the spit out of his eye and
lights his cigarette.

EXT. OUTSIDE A CONVENIENCE STORE—DUSK

A semi-busy Stop-and-Shop. Neon beer and cigarette advertisements glow in the windows.

Doug, wearing a black dress shirt and black slacks, stands outside, smoking by a stand-up ashtray beside his best friend ERIC.

Eric (late-twenties, blonde hair, and wearing a blinding purple dress shirt with gaudy bright blue slacks) is holding a case of light beer in his hands.

>   DOUG

>   You don't match, dude.

>   ERIC

>   Piss off. I dress the way I
>   want to.

>   DOUG

>   But you look like shit. How
>   are you gonna get some
>   pussy if you look like your
>   mother's color blind?

>   ERIC

>   Very funny.

DOUG (loud)

Do you have any weed? CAN
YOU GET SOME MARIJUANA?

Eric nervously looks around.

ERIC

(soft)

I don't, but we can always
go hang with Ras Oray. He
always has the good-good.

DOUG

Think he's home?

ERIC

He's slack—he's always
home.

DOUG

How can he afford being a
hermit?

ERIC

You don't want to know.

EXT. RAS ORAY'S HOME—NIGHT.

Doug and Eric stand in front of a
duplex with the numbers 9437 above the

door. Eric, still holding the case of beer in his hand, pushes the doorbell and we hear that the ring is the first nine notes of Beethoven's *Fur Elise.*

The door opens, and RAS ORAY, a black Rastafarian in his late thirties, is standing before them. He is wearing a worn Bob Marley T-shirt and baggy, camouflage cargo shorts. Thin, tight dreadlocks protrude from a bandana on his forehead and extend below his waist. When he smiles, two gold teeth gleam.

                    RAS ORAY

               (thick Caribbean accent)

          Welcome, friends. Welcome.

INT. RAS ORAY'S LIVING ROOM

Posters of reggae bands cover the walls of Ras Oray's small apartment. The fuzzy couches are zebra-striped. A large Jamaican flag hides the ceiling. An entertainment center with two turntables, a TV, and a stereo line the back wall.

Doug and Eric plop down on the couch as Ras puts a vinyl record on the left side of his dual turntables. The needle strikes the record with a POP, and SOFT JAZZ fills the room.

Ras joins Eric and Doug on the couch.

> ERIC

> Beer, Ras?

> RAS ORAY

> No, mon—I never touch da stuff. Poison to your soul and mind. I believe in burnin' da herb; now that's good medicine for your vibrations. Too bad I'm all out.

> DOUG

> For how long?

> RAS ORAY

> Maybe till Tuesday.

> DOUG

> Damn.

> ERIC

> It's all good. I brought alcohol.

Eric opens a can of beer and takes a long pull from it. Doug holds out his hands.

> DOUG
>
> Toss me one, cat. Damn, I
> wish I had some dope. I
> can't stand dry days.

> RAS ORAY
>
> Not dat important. Just
> another thing to pass time.
> So what's new you, guys?

> ERIC
>
> I finally became a twelfth-
> level dungeon master. Took
> a bunch of hours rolling
> dice. I'm trying to piece
> together a new quest. Got
> the layout for an entire
> realm and several side
> quests mapped out.

The room falls silent for a BEAT.

> ERIC
>
> I guess you guys aren't
> into roll playing.

> DOUG
>
> I'm trying to catch AIDS.

> ERIC

That's fucking sick—what do
you mean 'I'm trying to
catch AIDS?'

                DOUG

        (distant)

Something Sam said to me…

        ERIC

Really done, huh? You were
with that girl a while.

                DOUG

Seven months—the longest
relationship I've ever had.

        ERIC

That's really not that
long, cat.

        RAS ORAY

Any chance of you gettin'
back up wit' her?

                DOUG

No. It's over.

        ERIC

In seven months, how many
times did you cheat on her?

22

                    DOUG

Oh, Christ… Nineteen times.

                    RAS ORAY

Nineteen times! You *are*
trying to get sick. You're
still young—take care of
yourself, boy. Respect your
body because it's like a
god. It's all you got.

                    ERIC

Are you careful? Do you use
protection?

                    DOUG

Most of the time.

                    RAS ORAY

Most da time? You need ta
do it all da time

                    ERIC

He's bullshitting us, Ras.
No one's that stupid to do
such a dead fuck thing.
He's just trying to get a
reaction outta us.

                    RAS ORAY

        I 'ope he is, mon. 'ope he
        is.

                    DOUG

        Hold up, guys. Is it really
        such a bad idea? Think
        about it: why are people so
        afraid of loose sex?

Eric and Ras Oray exchange glances.

                    DOUG

        Because of whatever is out
        there, lurking in the bush.
        If you embrace disease,
        then sex has no boundaries.
        You become free to do
        whatever with whomever you
        want. I think it's an
        erotic notion.

Eric and Ras Oray are quiet.

                    ERIC

        EEEEK. It sounds like a
        turn-off to me. What's sexy
        about being sick?

                    DOUG

        Imagine you're having the

fuck of your life and in the back of your thoughts, you know that this is the one. You think, *this is the monster that's going to get* **me**. Or, when you're giving the time to some unsuspecting slut, you know that *you* have power over the rest of her life. Do you wear the condom? Do you take her life? One hell of a rush, man.

ERIC

There are better ways to catch a buzz, man. Besides, the way you live, you won't be alive long enough to catch AIDS.

RAS ORAY

Eric's right. Slow down, Doug.

DOUG

All this sex talk and not a woman in sight.

                    ERIC

          Is that all you can think
          about? Is there any depth
          in here?

                    DOUG

          Sex, drugs, and rock and
          roll, daddy-o. I'm no
          Buddhist; I embrace
          pleasure and passion. There
          is plenty of time in death
          not to feel alive.

                    ERIC

          Catch AIDS and you'll know
          all about that.

Doug and Eric glare at each other.

                    RAS ORAY

          Do you two want to catch a
          meal? Cheese steaks or
          pizza, perhaps?

                    DOUG

          I wanna go to a club, shake
          it with some dames.

Ras Oray gets up and stops the
turntable. The RECORD SLOWLY STOPS
SPINNING.

                    RAS ORAY

          You're killin' me, bro. I'm
          starving. You're welcome to
          join me for dinner
          festivities.

Eric hops up off the couch.

                    ERIC

          Sounds good—Fatty's?

                    RAS ORAY

          Sounds like a winner, mon.
          How 'bout you? Are you
          coming, Doug?

                    DOUG

          Nah, I'm not hungry. Why
          don't you two meet me at
          the club later? I bet I can
          score some smoke out there.

                    ERIC

          That's a plan. See you at
          the Mozzy later.

Doug gets up and Eric shakes his hand
firmly.

RAS ORAY

Keep da peace, free da
peace.

Ras Oray embraces Doug in a tight bear
hug, lifting him off the ground a few
inches.

EXT. OUTSIDE THE MOZZY—NIGHT.

Loud HOUSE MUSIC pours from the club
as Doug waits in a long line in front
of the ticket booth.

JANESSA, a blonde twenty-six-year-old
dressed in plastic raver clothes, cuts
the line to stand next to Doug.

Underneath the fluorescent black
lights, Janessa's glow-in-the-dark
jewelry shines in radiant colors as
she chews on a lollypop. She's
constantly fiddling with the strap of
her fuzzy, glowing purse.

JANESSA

How's it going, sexy?

DOUG

Janessa, I heard you were
dead. What happened?

JANESSA

Trippy, man. I ate some bad acid, but I didn't die. I wanted to try and jump off the pier, but my roommate got 911 on the phone pretty quick. They made me sit in life management for two fucking weeks. No cigarettes, no beer, no weed—I thought I was gonna crack. By the way, got a cigarette?

DOUG

Sure.

Doug pulls out his silver cigarette case and hands Janessa a cigarette. She lights up with a small, glowing butane lighter. She reaches in her fuzzy purse and pulls out two glow sticks then cracks them. As they come to life, she dances with them.

DOUG

If I knew you were in the hospital, I would have visited.

JANESSA

They wouldn't let anybody
see me, said I might just
be getting more drugs. Who
told you I was dead?

DOUG

I just heard it through
whispers. I haven't bought
any coke since.

JANESSA

Damn. Did ya crash hard?

DOUG

Not too bad. I've been
through much worse. I'm not
an everyday user, just
once-in-a-while.

Janessa stops dancing and moves a
little closer to Doug.

JANESSA

Hey, I heard you and Sam
are splits.

DOUG

Man, news travels fast in
this town. I can't take a
sideways piss without the

whole world knowing.

JANESSA

Tell me about it. So is it true? Is it *finally* over, or is it just more bullshit that the whispers scream?

DOUG

It's for real. We're done.

JANESSA

Yeah, right. You gotta stick to your guns this time, buddy. So are you coming over later?

DOUG

I'm not sure. I'm trying to score some smoke.

JANESSA

Well if you are feeling lucky, stop on by, stud. Don't forget, Okay?

DOUG

How could I? You live a block away.

Janessa gives Doug a little peck on the cheek and moves forward to cut ahead in another spot in line. Doug just shakes his head as he watches her work her mojo.

INT. INSIDE THE MOZZY—MINUTES LATER.

The HOUSE MUSIC is louder. Brilliant, multicolored lights sweep across the crowded club. Through the flashing strobes and glow stick trails, people gyrate on the dance floor and crowd the bar.

At the bar, Doug sips on a cocktail, talking to a well-dressed DRUNK in his late thirties sitting next to him. The drunk is totally wasted; through his thick slur, he can barely keep centered on the barstool.

DOUG

No smoke, huh?

DRUNK

SSSShit, I haven't smoked pot in ten years.

DOUG

Why did you quit?

The drunk puts his glass to his lips and spills some beverage across the bar.

                    DRUNK

          Got in the way of my
          drinking.

                    DOUG

          Oh.

An annoyed BARTENDER dressed in a white tuxedo shirt and black slacks comes over to clean up the mess.

                    DRUNK

          Say, buddy, can you lend me
          a couple of bucks so I can
          get a beer?

                    BARTENDER

          I'm sorry, sir. We can't
          serve you anymore. It's
          time to go.

                    DRUNK

          But I helped build this
          fucking place.

                    BARTENDER

          I don't care. I said you've
          had enough, and now it's
          time to go.

                    DRUNK

          Son of a bitch, I'm a
          veteran. I risked my life
          for this country, for your
          freedoms. Goddamn punk
          telling me what to do.

The drunk slides off the barstool and
makes it four stumbling steps before
collapsing on the edge of the dance
floor. Some nearby onlookers pick him
up and start hauling him towards the
exit.

                    The bartender shakes his
                    head.

                    BARTENDER

          That asshole's here every
          other week when he gets
          paid. Every other week, we
          have to drag him out. Not a
          word of truth comes out his
          damned mouth. If he weren't
          such a good tipper, I'd

tell security to stop him
at the door.

Eric appears from the crowd
with his wallet in his hand
and claims the seat vacated
by the drunk.

                    ERIC

There he is. Caught AIDS
yet?

The bartender's eyes widen.

                    DOUG

You can be a total prick,
ya know that?

                    BARTENDER
                (to Eric)

Do you have ID?

Eric pulls out his ID from his wallet
and hands it to the bartender.

                    ERIC

Yes, I do. I'll have a
lemon drop shot and a
jungle piss on the rocks,
please.

                    BARTENDER

No problem, sir. I'll be
right back.

The bartender hands Eric
back his ID and mixes the
drinks.

                    ERIC

Find anything?

                    DOUG

        Not yet. Where did
Ras go?

                    ERIC

He's somewhere in the crowd
looking for the diggity-
dank. Ras will probably
score. He's got the spirit
world on his side. Any
pretty ladies out there?

                    DOUG

This hasn't been my night.
Every girl I've tried to
buy a drink for
respectfully declines. The
only promising prospect for

                    36

some good loving later on
has been from Janessa.

                ERIC

Janessa. If you're serious
about catching HIV or
something, she's the way to
go.

                DOUG

What do mean by that?

                ERIC

Aw, come on. That girl is
dirty. She fucks everyone.

                DOUG

Have you fucked her?

                ERIC

Well, no I haven't.

                DOUG

        Then she hasn't
fucked everyone.

They laugh as the bartender brings the
drinks.

                BARTENDER

Sixteen-fifty, please.

Eric pulls the money out of his wallet and pays the bartender. Eric puts his wallet away as the bartender helps another customer.

                ERIC

I can't believe it...Janessa. Why diddle her when you could have them?

                DOUG

Who?

                ERIC

Those twins.

Eric points to the other side of the bar where IDENTICAL TWINS talk to each other. One is drinking a tall daiquiri and smoking a cigarette while the other twirls her long, straight hair in her fingers.

Doug and Eric watch them a BEAT, sipping on their drinks.

                DOUG

Twins.

ERIC

That's one for each of us.

Doug shoots Eric a look.

DOUG

Or two for me.

They laugh as Ras Oray joins them. He doesn't have a chance to speak when the bartender appears in front of them.

BARTENDER

For you, dude?

RAS ORAY

Nothing, thank you—never touch da stuff.

The bartender EXITS to help someone else.

DOUG

Did ya score?

RAS ORAY

'Dis town is dryer than a sidewinder's asshole. All I

could find is da ecstasy
crap. Some powdered molly
that the shade tree chemist
couldn't even press into
pills.

ERIC

Garbage. People will put
anything in their bodies.
Take fast food, for
example. Have you seen that
documentary where—

DOUG

How much?

RAS ORAY

What—how much does it cost,
or how much can I get?

DOUG

Both.

RAS ORAY

Fifty-five dollars per gram
and there's only two.

ERIC

Fifty-five dollars?

                    DOUG

That shylock motherfucker.

                    RAS ORAY

Just reporting. No need to
shoot the word-bringer

                    DOUG

I guess I have no choice
but to bite. Can you hook
it up?

                    RAS ORAY

I can arrange it.

                    DOUG

I think it's fucking
expensive, but I'll take
them both. Damn, I wish I
had some smoke.

Doug reaches into his back pocket and
pulls out a wad of twenty-dollar
bills. Ras eyes light up at the sight
of all the money.

                    DOUG

Here's a hundred and twenty

ANTHONY S. BUONI

dollars—keep ten for your
effort, Ras.

RAS ORAY

Thank you, mon. Shit should
be good, I know 'dis guy
real well.

Ras disappears into the crowd.

DOUG

For a hundred and twenty
dollars, this better not be
bunk.

ERIC

I can't believe you just
paid that much for designer
drugs.

DOUG

There's no weed around. I
gotta have something.

ERIC

You're almost a junkie,
Doug. Doesn't that bother
you?

DOUG

I'm not a junkie. I'm just
someone who enjoys life.

ERIC

Denial: the first stage.

DOUG

Hey, I use drugs
spiritually. It gets me in
touch with the gods and
goddesses.

ERIC

And that would be
justification. There is
nothing religious about
consuming intoxicants to
get twisted. Just keep on
digging, my friend. Slide
down that slippery slope.
There are plenty of support
groups waiting for you when
you hit rock bottom.

DOUG

Fuck you, man. You're no
saint. You fucking drink
all the time. How is that
different than any of my
bad habits?

ERIC

>Hey, look. Those twins are
>coming this way.

We see the twins, PAMELA and SHELIA,
walking empty-handed towards Doug and
Eric.

Shelia, drinking and smoking earlier,
is wearing a black leather short skirt
and a skimpy cut off top. A small
black purse dangles from her right
shoulder. She is in her mid-twenties
and has short black hair.

Pamela, more conservatively dressed,
is wearing black slacks and a tight T-
shirt that has "GOOD GIRL" in sparkly
lettering on it. Around her left wrist
is a plastic glow-in-the-dark
bracelet.

The twins stop right next to Doug and
Eric, both smiling.

DOUG

>Hey, girls, want a drink?
>It's on me if you're
>interested on staying for a
>little while.

PAMELA

No, thanks. But we'll stay
a while.

                    SHELIA

I'll take a white Russian.

                    DOUG

                    (to bartender)

White Russian for the nice
lady.

Shelia hands her ID to the bartender
and he examines it for a BEAT and then
hands it back.

                    BARTENDER

Coming right up.

The bartender leaves to mix the drink.

                    ERIC

So where are you girls
from?

                    PAMELA

Tennessee. But we live here
now.

                    DOUG

What part?

SHELIA

Gatlinburg.

DOUG

I've been there—what a
tourist trap.

SHELIA

So is this town.

ERIC

Hey, Panama City has
beautiful beaches.

PAMELA

Gatlinburg has beautiful
mountains.

DOUG

She's got a point, ass
lips.

SHELIA

Ass lips?

ERIC

He thinks that's funny.

                    DOUG

              (lighting a cigarette)

         It's fucking hilarious.

Ras Oray appears out of the crowd and
pulls Doug to the side.

                  RAS ORAY

              Here's da cigarettes you
              wanted.

Ras hands Doug an open pack of
cigarettes.

                    DOUG

              Thanks. I really appreciate
              it, Ras.

                  RAS ORAY

              No worries. I'll be at da
              house in an hour. I need to
              take care of a couple of
              tings. You're welcome to
              stop by if tings start
              getting weird, mon.

                    DOUG

         All right. Thanks, bro. I

might be by later.

RAS ORAY

Take care of yourself and
drink lots of water.

Ras and Doug embrace.

Ras makes his way out, snaking through
the crowd.

Doug returns to the conversation with
the twins. Shelia has her drink, and
Doug peels off the bartender a few
bills.

DOUG

Keep the change.

BARTENDER

Thanks.

The bartender EXITS.

DOUG

(to twins)

My name is Doug. This is my
good buddy, Eric.

SHELIA

This is Pamela. I'm Shelia.

                    PAMELA

Hi.

                    ERIC

It's a pleasure to meet
you. Are you sure you don't
want a drink Pamela? I'm
buying.

                    PAMELA

Sorry. I'm the designated
driver tonight. Actually,
I'm the DD every night. I
don't like getting too
messed up. I wind up
feeling like crap the next
morning.

                    SHELIA

It's my personal mission to
go out like a rock star
tonight.

Shelia takes a long sip of her white
Russian and licks her lips.

                    SHELIA

Whoo! That's tasty. This
bartender knows how to

treat a girl.

DOUG

Girl? You're no girl. What
I see before me is a
beautiful woman.

PAMELA

Do you believe this guy?
I've heard better come-ons
from Disney channel teeny-
boppers.

SHELIA

I don't know. I think he's
kind of cute. Maybe even a
little charming.

DOUG

I'm a real nice guy.

ERIC

Until you get to know him.

SHELIA

I think he's got to worry
about me more than I have
to fear him.

DOUG

Oh, is that so?

PAMELA

Stop it, Shelia. You are
embarrassing yourself.

SHELIA

Oh, piss off. You're not
ruining my good time. Why
don't go find a Bible and
save the soul of the
unwashed masses or
something?

ERIC

Hey, hey—easy ladies. Pam,
would you like to dance.
This song is dope, and I
feel like grooving.

Pamela glares at her sister.

PAMELA

Sure. I can't stand to see
this crap anyways.

Eric offers up a hand and takes her
into the gyrating crowd.

SHELIA

Alone at last. I swear,

you'd never guess we were
sisters. She's always on my
ass about the way I live,
but, fuck, it's my life.
She can go and live in her
Sunday school wet dream
till she drops, but I wanna
live.

                    DOUG

Amen, sister. My friends
get on me, too. I think
it's because they can't
keep up.

Shelia laughs.

The bartender returns.

                    BARTENDER

Refills?

Doug exchanges a glance with Shelia.

                    DOUG

Absolutely, darling.

The bartender EXITS to mix the drinks.

                    DOUG

So, do you party?

SHELIA

What do you mean?

DOUG

Do you roll?

SHELIA

Are you holding?

DOUG

What about that sister of yours? Does she party?

SHELIA

You have a lot of nerve asking me that.

DOUG

What?

SHELIA

I don't think she would be into the threesome thing.

Doug pauses and then Shelia gets a strange smile on her face.

SHELIA

How many pills do you have?

                    DOUG

        A few, but they're not on
        me.

                    SHELIA

        Pam doesn't get high.

                    DOUG

        Oh. Well, I figured that.

Shelia leans close to Doug's ear.

                    SHELIA

        I do.

                    DOUG

        Want to walk on the beach?

                    SHELIA

        That sounds like a great
        idea.

                    DOUG

        What about your sister?

                    SHELIA

        What about your friend?

Doug chuckles.

                    DOUG

He's a big boy. I think he
can find his way home.

                    SHELIA

Well, Pam's a pest, and I
think she has church at the
crack of who gives a fuck.
She's driving, and I told
her not to wait up for me.

                    DOUG

Smart move.

Shelia gets up, holding her hand out.
Doug rises and they leave without
getting their drinks.

EXT. BEACH—TEN MINUTES LATER

Doug and Shelia walk arm-in-arm in the
crashing surf. Doug is carrying both
of their shoes. They stop and engage
in a long, passionate kiss.
Afterwards, Shelia reaches in her
purse and pulls out a pint of tequila.

                    SHELIA

Wanna get warm?

Doug accepts the bottle. He opens the
lid and takes a big swallow from the
glass flask. He passes it to Shelia
who turns the bottle up and chugs a
quarter of its contents. They open-
mouth kiss again.

                    SHELIA

               (breathing heavy)

          Where do we have to go to
          get the pills?

                    DOUG

          Are you ready to drop now?

Shelia kisses Doug's neck as he rubs
his hands up her side and onto her
breasts. They lock lips. She slides
her hands into the back of his pants,
grabbing his ass. Doug drops the shoes
into the breaking waves and wraps his
arms around her.

                    DOUG

          Let's get someplace dry.

They walk onto a sand dune and Doug
pulls out the pack of cigarettes. He
opens up the box and shakes the two
pills out onto his hand. Shelia
smiles. He places one between his

thumb and forefinger and slides it
into Shelia's mouth.

                    DOUG

          Chew it up.

                    SHELIA

          I know how to take drugs,
          Doug. This isn't my first
          time, ya know. Drop with
          me?

                    DOUG

          Of course.

Doug pops the other pill into his
mouth and chews. They make disgusted
faces.

                    SHELIA

          Tastes like shit.

                    DOUG

          That's funny.

                    SHELIA

          What?

                    DOUG

          That tequila tasted like

piss.

          SHELIA

We need to find somewhere
safe.

          DOUG

I hear ya. I'm going to
blow the fuck up, and I
don't think this public
beach is the right place.

          SHELIA

My apartment is near. We
could walk.

          DOUG

What do we do about your
sister?

          SHELIA

We don't live together. Is
your friend Eric some kind
of psycho, or is he going
to be sweet to my sister.

          DOUG

Fuck him.

> SHELIA
>
> I'm serious, Doug. Is he a
> total freak or what?

> DOUG
>
> He's painfully normal, if
> there is such a thing. And
> besides, you got more to
> worry about me than she
> does him.

They give each other a sloppy kiss and
start walking.

> SHELIA
>
> We'll see about that.

INT. SHELIA'S APARTMENT—THIRTY MINUTES
LATER

We see the front door swing open.

Shelia and Doug stumble in, necking.
They fall to the ground and continue
kissing halfway in the open doorway.
Shelia rips open Doug's black dress
shirt and drags her fingernails down
his chest, leaving red scratch marks.

As she fumbles with his pants, he
tears off her skimpy, cut-off top and

reveals her chest. Shelia gets Doug's
pants open and pulls them down. Doug
is not wearing underwear. Doug's hands
slide up Shelia's short, leather
skirt, exposing her hips.

SHELIA

Now… Put it in me now…

DOUG

I don't have a condom—

SHELIA

Just fuck me, Doug. Fuck me
hard.

INT. SHELIA'S BEDROOM—LATER

Shelia's plain room plain has a bed, a
nightstand with a purple lava lamp and
a radio, and a small pile of CDs
stacked next to the radio. Scattered
clothes litter the floor. Soft NEW
WAVE music fills the room as Doug and
Shelia bask in the afterglow of sex.

Doug and Shelia smoke cigarettes while
sharing a can of beer. Sprawled out
side-by-side on Shelia's bed, black,
satin covers partly cover their

entwined limbs.

Hair frazzled, they drip with perspiration.

> DOUG

Sex smells awesome.

> SHELIA

Yeah.

Doug rolls on his side and faces Shelia.

> DOUG

Do you have any more booze?

> SHELIA

No, this is the last beer.

> DOUG

Damn.

> SHELIA

I'm still rolling. I was peeking about the time we got back.

> DOUG

My pill is wearing off.

Maybe we should try to cop some more.

SHELIA

I don't know. I feel pretty damn good. I think I'm gonna be sore tomorrow.

Doug snickers.

SHELIA

Shut up—you were kind of rough.

DOUG

You loved it.

Shelia rolls over and kisses Doug.

DOUG

That's funny.

SHELIA

What's that?

DOUG

Tea bagging and swashbuckling.

SHELIA

Tea bagging?

DOUG

Yeah, that's when you dip
your balls into a girl's
mouth so she can suck on
them.

SHELIA

Jesus, now I'm afraid to
ask about swashbuckling.

DOUG

That's when a girl sucks
two dicks at the same time.
It's like a sword fight
going on in her mouth.

SHELIA

Gross. Are you trying to
tell me you have an oral
fetish

DOUG

You don't think that's hot?
Maybe hott with two T's?

SHELIA

Not really.

DOUG

I thought you liked sex.

SHELIA

I love it, but that doesn't mean I want two cocks in my mouth at once.

DOUG

So how do you feel about one in your mouth, one in your cunt, and one in your ass?

Shelia sits up and slaps Doug.

SHELIA

You pervert, I can't believe you just said that.

DOUG

What? Don't go all holier-than-thou on me, sister. **You** just let me screw you without a condom.

SHELIA

I—I—

DOUG

That's right. Why be
bashful now?

Shelia wraps herself tight in the
covers.

SHELIA

I guess I got caught up in
the moment.

DOUG

It's amazing isn't it?
There's no telling what we
might have shared.

SHELIA

What are you talking about?

DOUG

I could have caught
something from you and
vice-versa.

SHELIA

Why are you saying such

awful things? Do you have
something?

DOUG

Hopefully.

SHELIA

I can't believe this shit.
You're serious aren't you?

DOUG

I can explain it to you if
you would like. Where are
you going?

Shelia gets out of bed, keeping
herself wrapped in the covers.

SHELIA

I don't want to hear
whatever crackpot logic
you're cooking up. Damn it,
I liked you, Doug.

DOUG

I figured that by how easy
you were.

SHELIA

Get out. You can't stay

here tonight.

DOUG

Aw, come one, Shelia. What
did you think this was? Did
you think you were throwing
some magic pussy at me,
that I was going to cum so
hard that my heart was
gonna squirt out my cock
and into your arms?

SHELIA

Fuck you.

DOUG

Again? If you insist, sugar
tits.

SHELIA

I'm not fucking kidding.
Get out.

Doug rolls out of bed and picks up his
clothes from the floor.

SHELIA

I better not be sick.

Doug pulls on the last of his
garments.

                    DOUG

          Does this mean you don't
          want my phone number?

                    SHELIA

          Get out.

Shelia begins to push Doug to the
front door.

                    DOUG

          Are you sure you don't want
          me to stay? We could—

                    SHELIA

          (opening the front door)

          Thanks for the night, Doug,
          but I don't ever want to
          see you again.

Before Doug can get a word in
edgewise, Shelia shoves him out the
door and slams it shut.

EXT. OUTSIDE SHELIA'S HOUSE—CONTINUING

The door slams.

Doug is outside alone.

CRICKETS CHIRP as Doug walks toward the street.

                    DOUG

          Mission accomplished.

INT. NICK'S HOUSE—THE NEXT EVENING

Doug, dressed in a white, short-sleeved button-up shirt and black slacks, is sitting on a blue couch.

Doug rubs his thumb against his gold Zippo in his right hand as NICK (early twenties, balding, dressed in a green bathrobe and flannel pajama bottoms) cracks his knuckles.

                    DOUG

          So after she threw me out,
          I went to the strip club
          and burned some dollar
          bills. Wound up meeting
          this guy named Griff who
          claimed to be a pimp, but I
          didn't have enough loot to
          purchase his high-dollar

hooker.

NICK

You would have bought a
hooker?

DOUG

I've never done it before.
It seems like an experience
worth having.

NICK

I don't think that buying
sex is an experience, but
then again, selling weed
gets my rocks off.

Nick puts a large, elaborate,
glass water bong with three
chambers to his lips and sparks
up. The BONG BUBBLES and the
glass chambers fill up with
thick smoke.

DOUG

How is it that every time
this town is dry, you still
have smoke?

Nick pulls the slide out of the bong
and inhales the smoke, immediately

erupting into a coughing fit.

Doug laughs.

> NICK
>
> Don't ask. Shit, even
> through the water that
> grass is still harsher than
> a Martian sunrise. Hey,
> man, Ras Oray was by last
> night looking for the
> chronic, and he was worried
> about some madness you were
> blowing.

> DOUG
>
> What did he say?

> NICK
>
> Don't worry about it, man.
> It was probably just a load
> of crap, anyway.

> DOUG
>
> Come on, cat. You just
> can't leave me hanging by
> an unfurled pubic hair.
> Tell me more.

Nick is quiet for a BEAT.

                    NICK

          He said something about you
          and AIDS. It's stupid. I
          shouldn't have said
          anything.

Nick passes the bong to Doug and looks
around the room nervously.

                    DOUG

          So?

Doug lights the bong and begins to
fill it up with smoke.

                    NICK

          Is this static real? Do you
          really mean it?

          Doug nods as the BONG
          BUBBLES and the chambers
          fill with smoke.

                    NICK

          What the fuck is the point?
          It just doesn't make sense.
          Why the attempt? Why would
          you do such a thing?

Doug exhales a large cloud of
smoke.

DOUG

Why not? There's no way to explain it. It's easy to get lost in the passion. My heart beats fast, I can hardly breathe. The touching, tasting, rubbing— I live for flesh pressed against flesh. If I can heighten the intensity of the moment, it just makes the orgasm that much better. I take drugs, and when I climax, my world rattles. When I'm drunk, I can screw for hours before losing my wad. Sometimes, my cock gets so fucking hard, I can't see straight.

NICK

OK, OK…I get the point.

DOUG

I like to explore sex. When I first heard myself say it, I wasn't serious about catching the disease, but, now, it makes sense. I need to welcome it because it's the path I'm on.

> Eventually, there's no turning back. I might as well enjoy myself before I reach that point of no return.

Doug pulls out his silver cigarette case and removes a smoke. He rolls the square in his fingers as the room falls quiet a BEAT.

                    NICK

> It sounds like you've given this a lot of thought. If that's what you want, Doug, then that's what you want. Have you ever met Jesus?

                    DOUG

What?

Doug lights his cigarette with his Zippo.

                    NICK

> When I'm feeling lost in my life, and it happens often, I pray to Jesus Christ for protection, forgiveness, and understanding. It helps me get over the noise that threatens my existence.

DOUG

It's not that simple for
me, Nick. I hate to say
this, but I don't think
Jesus listens to me.

Nick places his left hand on Doug's
right shoulder.

NICK

My friend, Jesus is always
listening.

DOUG

I don't think he has time
for this old sinner. Let me
tell you a story: when I
was twelve-years-old, I
wanted this boss mountain
bike. It was mucho
expensive, and my parents
told me they couldn't
afford such a thing. A
moment of genius struck me.
I asked Jesus for the bike.
Six months, I prayed for
the damned thing. For *six
months,* I prayed three
times a day and never got
it. That's when it hit me.
Praying to Jesus for things

was like asking Santa for presents. Totally meaningless.

                NICK

I don't think that's quite how it works. You pray to God for spiritual enlightenment—to help pave your path. It's not for something you expect in return.

A DOORBELL RINGING interrupts the conversation.

                NICK

One moment, let me see who the fuck *this* is.

Nick gets off the couch and opens the front door. Standing at the entrance is Janessa, wearing a yellow, long-sleeved T-shirt and baggy, corduroy pants. Her fuzzy purse hangs from her right shoulder, and she slides her hand up and down the strap.

                JANESSA

Nick, I am so glad to see

you.

Janessa's eyes catch Doug sitting in the living room as she embraces Nick.

                    JANESSA

          DOUG. What's up, sexy?

                     NICK

          Hey, Janessa, come on in.

Janessa ENTERS. As Nick shuts the door, she sets her fuzzy purse on the ground. Doug snuffs out his cigarette in a round, ceramic ashtray on the center of Nick's coffee table.

                     DOUG

          Sit over here, baby.

Janessa plops down on the couch beside Doug.

Nick settles into his original seat.

                     NICK

          What brings you my way?

                     DOUG

          She knew I was hanging

around today.

                    JANESSA

          That's funny. Can I hit the
          bong?

Janessa rests her head on Doug's
shoulder and bats her eyelashes.

                     NICK

          Go ahead—I don't think it's
          cashed yet.

Janessa takes a large bong hit and
exhales the smoke.

                    JANESSA

          Nice smoke. Everybody is
          dry around town. How is it
          you still have smoke?

Janessa puts the bong on Nick's coffee
table.

                     DOUG

          He's not talking, so don't
          ask.

Nick crosses his arms and smiles.

                     NICK

Never doubt the power of a
Jedi Spirit.

Nick cracks his knuckles
and stretches his arms into
the air, placing his still
clasped hands behind his
head.

DOUG

So what are you up to,
Janessa?

JANESSA

Actually, Doug, I was
wondering if you guys knew
where I could score some
powder?

NICK

Damn it, why do you put
that shit in your body?
It'll stop your heart one
day.

JANESSA

Fuck that. If ya die doing
something ya love, what's
the big deal?

DOUG

ANTHONY S. BUONI

That's what I'm singing.

NICK

I guess I just live my life
differently.

JANESSA

I'll say. You're a Goddamn
drug dealer.

NICK

Don't use blasphemy.

JANESSA

Then, what do you mean 'you
live your life
differently?'

NICK

I'll admit, I'm no saint,
but I try to take care of
myself. I seldom ever
drink. I don't smoke
cigarettes. I don't sleep
around, and fuck-fuck-fuck
a bunch of cocaine. I don't
mean to sound preachy but
why are you two so self-
destructive?

JANESSA

Everybody dies, so screw
it—enjoy your life while ya
still have it.

Janessa traces circles on the
mouthpiece of the bong with her
pointer finger.

> NICK

I just don't understand.

> JANESSA

You're bumming me out,
Nick. I guess I'll catch ya
later.

> DOUG

Man, you're leaving
fast. One bong toke and
that's it?

> JANESSA

Why don't you come with me,
Doug? We could hit a bar or
something.

> DOUG

Sounds cool. Well, I guess
I'm outta here, Nick.
Thanks for the buzz, man.

Doug and Nick shake hands.

NICK

No problem. Just take care
of yourselves. I don't
wanna see any of my friends
getting hurt doing
something stupid.

INT. BAR—THIRTY MINUTES LATER

Inside the small "locals only" bar,
CLASSIC ROCK plays from a flashing
jukebox. There are few tables, and a
lone dartboard rests against the back
wall. A sign dangling from the only
pool table reads "OUT OF ORDER" in
huge red letters.

Doug and Janessa are drinking mixed
drinks from clear plastic cups. They
are the only people in the bar except
for the BARTENDER, wearing a white
Corona shirt and brown slacks, who is
stocking liquor bottles and washing
glass ashtrays.

DOUG

So I went to her place, and
we screwed around a little.

JANESSA

Was she fine? How were her
tits?

DOUG

They were all right. I
wouldn't put her in a porno
mag, but she looked okay.

JANESSA

How about me?

DOUG

What about you?

Janessa leans back in her seat.

JANESSA

Would you put me in a
whack-off magazine?

DOUG

I've never seen you naked.

Janessa pulls up her shirt and flashes
her breasts to Doug.

BARTENDER

> Hey, put your clothes back on.

Janessa laughs and replaces her shirt.

                    JANESSA

> Don't you worry, sugar. A little titty never hurt anyone. So?

                    DOUG

> They're nice. Sure, I'd put you in a magazine. I bet a lot of horny teenage boys would go blind 'cause of those.

Janessa leans forward, and with her elbows resting on the bar, clasps her chin with her right hand.

                    JANESSA

> So, what do you got?

                    DOUG

> What do ya mean?

                    JANESSA

> Pull it out—I wanna see if you're hung like a field mouse or a turtle.

DOUG

Who, exactly, has the
bigger dong in that
scenario?

BARTENDER

That's enough, dude. If you
expose yourself, you're
both outta here.

JANESSA

No fair.

DOUG

Don't worry, the one-eyed
monster is staying in the
dungeon for now.

A group of THREE LOCALS enters the
bar: JED is tall and dressed in all
black. FRANK, wearing a blue baseball
cap with a red "03", is dressed in
blue jeans and a dark blue T-shirt.
JASON is dressed in a white T-shirt
and is wearing tan slacks. They sit at
the other end of the bar, and the
bartender takes their drink orders.

JANESSA

Hey, I know those guys.

                    DOUG

                  (jealous)

I don't.

                  JANESSA

          Wait a sec, I'll be right
          back.

Janessa hops off her barstool and
walks over to the trio.

Eyeing them, Doug sips on his drink as
the three crowd around Janessa. After
a few BEATS, Janessa bounces back over
to Doug.

                  JANESSA

          Let me borrow fifty bucks.

                    DOUG

What?

                  JANESSA

          Just let me borrow the
          money. I promise I'll pay
          you back Monday.

                    DOUG

>   Okay…okay, here.

Doug reaches into his pocket and pulls
out his wad of money and his silver
cigarette case. He thumbs out fifty
dollars and hands it to Janessa.

>   JANESSA

>   Thanks, Doug, I swear I'll
>   pay you back.

Janessa rushes over to the guys, and
they all huddle close together.

The bartender, while by a corner sink,
drops a mug to the floor and GLASS
BREAKS.

>   JED

>   Just put that anywhere.

The bartender, blushing, cleans up the
mess.

Janessa returns to Doug's side,
grinning ear-to-ear.

>   JANESSA

>   I just heard a funny joke.

>   DOUG

Let's hear it.

JANESSA

What do you call a Scotsman with a hundred girlfriends?

DOUG

I donno. A stud?

JANESSA

A shepherd.

DOUG

Hey, I'm Scottish.

Janessa looks startled.

DOUG

It's okay, I thought it was funny, too. Jesus, talk about sexual deviancy. Say, what did you need all that cash for?

JANESSA

Just forget about it. So, is there any chance of you getting back with Sam? She was a good girl, ya know.

DOUG

No, we're through. I'm on a
mission now.

JANESSA

Really? What is your quest,
Sir Knight?

DOUG

Sexual freedom—I'm trying
to catch AIDS.

JANESSA

Are you kidding?

DOUG

No, it makes too much sense
to me now.

JANESSA

Cool.

DOUG

Cool? You're not upset?

Janessa shakes her head.

DOUG

ANTHONY S. BUONI

Everyone else I've told
freaks out.

JANESSA

I'm not like everyone else.
You should come over
tonight.

DOUG

Oh yeah, why is that?

JANESSA

So we can play with
needles.

DOUG

What?

JANESSA

I like to shoot up. It's
not something I want
everyone to know, but I
love the high. Really gets
me wet.

DOUG

I've never shot anything
before. What are you
taking?

JANESSA

Heroin and cocaine. Once in
a while oxys, roxys, or
xanax.

DOUG

How long have you been at
it?

JANESSA

A little over a year. To be
honest, I haven't always
been safe, either.

DOUG

Haven't been safe?

JANESSA

I've shared needles with
people.

DOUG

Do you know if you're
clean?

JANESSA

I don't know—I've been too

afraid to go to the free
clinic.

DOUG

Why? You seem so
nonchalant.

JANESSA

I donno. Maybe if I had any
diseases and people found
out, they wouldn't hang
with me anymore.

DOUG

Just because you have
something doesn't mean you
have to tell everybody
what's going on. I mean,
that's your business,
right?

JANESSA

So you're saying if you
caught AIDS, you would
spread it without telling
your partners?

DOUG

Why advertise? It's fun to
have an advantage in the

game.

                    JANESSA

Damn, Doug, that's
hardcore. So much for the
ideals of PLUR.

                    DOUG

PLUR?

                    JANESSA

That's raver-talk for
peace, love, unity, and
respect.

                    DOUG

Yeah, our generation's
pretty selfish. Were gonna
see another nuke dropped in
our lifetime, and I mean
the big one, mark my words.
People our age are crazy
enough to do it.

Janessa leans in close to Doug.

                    JANESSA

So what do ya say? My
place?

Doug thinks a BEAT and

leans in closer to Janessa.

DOUG

Why not, life's a series of experiences, right?

JANESSA

Right, we'll have a blast, Doug.

Doug turns his plastic cup back and gulps the rest of his drink. He drops a couple of dollars on the bar, flips open his cigarette case and pulls out a smoke.

They get up from the barstools and hug. Wrapping their arms around each other's waist, they make their way out.

JANESSA

(back turned)

Thanks, guys.

The bartender RINGS A BELL and drops Doug's money into a tip jar.

INT. JANESSA'S FLAT—LATER

Janessa's apartment is simple. An old blue couch faces a small TV tuned to static and propped up on an overturned milk crate. Next to the TV, a small boom box thumps TECHNO; upside-down CDs litter the brown carpet.

Janessa and Doug are in the nearby kitchen, hovering over a square mirror with white powder piled on it. Janessa chops the pile with a black credit card with bold red letters.

> DOUG
>
> You ever bought coke from that guy before?

> JANESSA
>
> Once or twice. The last stuff was fire.

Doug reaches for the pile but hesitates.

> DOUG
>
> Do you mind?

> JANESSA
>
> It's half your money, too.

Doug pinches the pile and tastes a couple of the white grains.

> DOUG
>
> Numbed me pretty quick. Tastes good.

> JANESSA
>
> Did ya wanna rip a rail first?

> DOUG
>
> Hell yeah, rack 'em up.

Janessa uses the credit card to line up two small rows of the powder as Doug pulls out his cash wad and rolls a hundred-dollar bill into a tube. He hands the homemade straw to Janessa. She puts one end into her nostril and snorts up one of the lines. She lifts her head up, pinching her nose.

> JANESSA
>
> Damn, that burns so good.

Janessa hands the straw to Doug who snorts his line. He tosses the rolled up bill onto the counter, and it starts to slightly unroll.

> DOUG

> *Damn*, that's good shit.

Janessa opens a drawer and pulls out a spoon with a carbon-scorched bottom and a pack of matches. She grabs a white candle from next to the sink and hands it to Doug along with the matches.

JANESSA

> Light this for me, I'll be right back.

Janessa EXITS.

Doug strikes the match and lights the wick. As he sets the glowing candle on the counter, Janessa returns with a handful of cotton balls.

She grabs a toothpick from a yellow, ceramic owl on the stove.

Janessa scoops up some of the powder with the corner of the credit card and pours it into the spoon.

She rests the spoon beside the sink and opens up and overhead cabinet, pulling out an eyedropper.

She turns on the faucet and sucks water from the falling stream with the eyedropper.

Janessa releases a couple of drops of water onto the spoon and stirs the mixture with the toothpick.

She hands the spoon over to Doug

JANESSA

Hold this—don't spill it.

Doug nods and takes the spoon. His hands shake, but he doesn't spill a drop.

Janessa reaches into the open cabinet and pulls out a syringe with a bright orange cap covering the tip.

JANESSA

I call this one Rex; he's still sharp, but I've used him twice. I got new ones too…in case he gets dull.

Janessa takes the spoon from Doug and holds it over the tip of the candle's dancing flame. After a BEAT, the contents begin to bubble and cook down.

Janessa puts the spoon on the counter and uncaps the syringe.

She rips a cotton ball and places half

of it into the spoon.

She inserts the tip of the needle into the soaked cotton ball then pulls up the plunger, sucking the fluid into the syringe.

> JANESSA
>
> You don't want air in the syringe—bubbles are bad.

> DOUG
>
> Intense.

Janessa holds the needle so the point is facing the ceiling and pushes the plunger slightly—the tip of the needle bleeds a few drops. She grips the needle between her teeth.

Janessa rolls up her sleeve; bruises dot her forearm.

> JANESSA
>
> (through clenched teeth)
>
> Sometimes I miss.

Doug nods.

Janessa unbuckles her belt.

Doug raises an eyebrow.

They chuckle as they exchange a glance.

Janessa wraps the belt around her upper arm, across her bicep. The veins along her arm bulge.

Janessa lines up the needle's point to one of the throbbing veins.

> JANESSA
>
> I have a girlfriend who's shot so long, she can't use her arm anymore. Now, she sticks herself in that hidden area between her toes. Sometimes she shoots up in her pussy.

> DOUG
>
> Ouch.

> JANESSA
>
> I don't ever wanna go that far.

Janessa sticks the needle into the crook of her arm and pulls a little blood into the syringe. Then, she pushes the plunger down. She pulls the needle out of her arm and loosens the belt.

Her mouth shivers.

She closes her eyes as they roll back.

> JANESSA
>
> (breathing heavy)
>
> Do you still want to?

Doug thinks a BEAT then nods his head.

> DOUG
>
> Let's do it. Get Rex ready
> for me, I'll be right back.
> I gotta take a piss.

> JANESSA
>
> You know where the bathroom
> is, right?

> DOUG
>
> I puked in it two years
> ago—St. Patrick's Day.
> Remember?

> JANESSA
>
> Yeah. God, I wanted to fuck
> you so bad that night. You
> were so hammered, I don't
> think you could have got it
> up even I shoved a dozen

                    prick pills up your ass.

                         DOUG

                    I wish you would play with
                    my butt. Be right back.

                         JANESSA

                    Well then, I'll tuck that
                    information away for later.
                    Remember, cowboy, if ya
                    shake it more than twice,
                    you're playing with it.

Janessa laughs as Doug walks down the
hall.

Janessa CHOPS the cocaine as Doug
shuts the bathroom door.

INT. JANESSA'S BATHROOM—CONTINUING

Doug URINATES and FLUSHES, the toilet
WHOOSHES as he puts down the seat
cover.

Doug goes over to the sink, littered
with make-up kits, plastic glow-in-
the-dark jewelry, a yellow toothbrush,
and watermelon hand soap. A half-
squeezed tube of toothpaste spills its
blue guts onto the left-hand side of

the sink.

Doug glances over to Janessa'a bathtub, stained with lime deposits and dark grease spots.

He uses the hand soap and turns on the sink, lathering his hands and rinsing them clean. He shuts off the faucet and searches for a towel. Unable to find one, he dries his hands in his armpits.

Doug looks at himself in the mirror fir a BEAT.

                    DOUG

          Here we go.

Doug EXITS.

INT. JANESSA'S KITCHEN—CONTINUING

Doug walks into the kitchen as Janessa fills the syringe with the spoon's contents.

                    JANESSA

               I'm not gonna give you the
               same amount of CCs as I
               just shot. I don't wanna
               hurt you, this being your

first time and all.

Janessa holds the needle up and flicks
it; a few drops leak from the point.

> DOUG
>
> Is that the same point you
> just used?

> JANESSA
>
> Yeah, this is Rex. Sure you
> don't want a clean one?

> DOUG
>
> I'm sure.

Janessa hands Doug her belt. Doug ties
it around his upper arm.

> JANESSA
>
> I love virgins—the first
> thing that's gonna happen
> is you're gonna hear
> freight trains screaming in
> your ears.

Doug nervously chuckles; his veins
protrude.

> JANESSA
>
> Give me your arm.

Doug holds out his arm and Janessa gently slides the needle tip into his arm. As he looks away, Janessa pulls a little of Doug's blood into the syringe and then pushes the plunger down.

Doug closes his eyes as she pulls the needle out of his arm and loosens the tourniquet.

Doug shudders when the high hits. Janessa giggles with delight.

He stumbles back.

Janessa crosses the counter, hugging Doug tight.

                    JANESSA

          Feel good?

                    DOUG

          Holy shit—

          Janessa nibbles on Doug's
          ear as he shakes and
          breaths heavy.

                    DOUG

          I've never felt anything
          like this before. You were

right about the trains…
It's almost like bells
ringing. How long does this
last, anyway?

JANESSA

Not long enough.

Doug opens his eyes and they stare at
each other a BEAT.

JANESSA

I've always liked you,
Doug.

Doug smiles and we can see his jaw
shivering.

DOUG

I don't like relationships.
They never work for me.

Janessa leans forward and kisses Doug
passionately.

JANESSA

How do you feel about just
having a little fun?

Doug leans in and they kiss again,

pulling at each other's clothes.

INT. JANESSA'S FLAT—THE NEXT MORNING

Janessa, wearing only a long, white T-shirt and sitting on her bed, fumbles through a stack of phone numbers written on various loose, multicolored pieces of paper.

Doug is sprawled next to her wearing only boxer shorts with hundreds of bright yellow smiley faces.

                    DOUG

          I hope I make it through
          work—I'm wired from the
          blow. What the fuck are you
          doing?

                    JANESSA

          Trying to figure out where
          I can score more coke. One
          of these fuckers has to
          have another eight ball.

DOUG

We just shot a bunch. I
need to chill out—come
down.

JANESSA

I want more. Damn it, why
is it that the only people
I know are assholes?

Doug laughs and hops out of bed. He
pulls his clothes on.

JANESSA

Where are you going?

DOUG

I gotta go take a shower
and get ready for work at
my bullshit job.

JANESSA

Are you still at Big
Burgers?

DOUG

Fucking shit work. This
time of year there is
barely any hours.

JANESSA

Where do you get the cash
for your extracurricular
hobbies?

DOUG

Don't ask. You know how
America is nowadays—gotta
have a hustle to keep a
head up. If my stupid job
wasn't such a turd, I
wouldn't have to cut
corners.

JANESSA

If you don't like it, why
don't you go back to school
and make something of
yourself?

DOUG

What in the hell would *I*
be? A doctor? An
accountant? A teacher? I
think not. Why waste the
time and money?

Doug pulls out his silver cigarette
case and puts a cigarette to his
mouth. Leaving it unlit, the cigarette
dangles from his lips.

JANESSA

May I have one of those?

Doug tosses her a smoke. She lights up from a blue Bic lighter on her nightstand.

JANESSA

Thanks.

DOUG

I guess I'll catch ya later.

Doug turns to leave.

JANESSA

Hey.

Doug stops and turns to face her.

DOUG

Yes, Janessa?

JANESSA

I've been thinking…

DOUG

Oh no…

JANESSA

Shut up.

DOUG

Sorry. And…

JANESSA

It's childish that I've
been afraid to get checked
out. I mean, what's there
to be afraid of, right?

DOUG

Everybody dies somehow.

JANESSA

I'm just saying, if there
ever was something wrong, I
could get help and take
care of myself.

DOUG

You can't be afraid of what
you are.

JANESSA

Thanks, Doug. Hey. I'm no
longer afraid.

                    DOUG

        Of what?

                    JANESSA

        Of being myself.

                    DOUG

        Glad to have helped.

                    JANESSA

        If I ever catch something,
        I'll let you know.

                    DOUG

        Thanks, baby.

Doug EXITS.

INT. RAS ORAY'S LIVING ROOM—LATER THAT
DAY

Ras Oray, wearing headphones, a shirt
covered in Jamaican flags, and baggy,
brown shorts, is mixing records on his
dual, Technics turntables. We hear
DEEP BREAKS as he gracefully combines
the two records.

Sam and Nick are on the zebra couch,

sharing a joint.

Nick is wearing a Grateful Dead tour shirt and cut-off jean shorts. Sam is wearing a red Simpson's shirt and black slacks.

> SAM
>
>> That movie was awesome. I can't believe I've never seen it. Donnie Darko is my personal hero.
>
> NICK
>
>> By the end of it, my mouth was like this:

Nick opens his mouth and leaves it dangling for a BEAT.

> SAM
>
>> Damn, Ras, that was an amazing mix.

Ras Oray turns around and smiles at her, revealing his gold teeth. Bobbing his head to the music, Ras Oray resumes his attention to the tables.

> NICK
>
>> So, you and Doug are finished, huh?

SAM

I caught the bastard
cheating on me. I suspected
he was up to no good a
couple of months ago, but I
had to catch him in the
act.

NICK

Did you walk in on him
banging another chick?

Sam shoots him a glare as she hits the
joint.

NICK

I'm sorry. I wasn't trying
to be insensitive—just
curious.

Sam exhales a cloud of grey
smoke.

SAM

No, I saw him at the Mozzy,
sucking face with some
bimbo. The fucking nerve.

Sam passes the joint to Nick.

SAM

And then ya know what he said to me when we got back to his house?

Nick shrugs as he tokes on the left-handed lucky.

                    SAM

          He told me he was trying to catch AIDS.

Nick erupts into a coughing fit; Ras Oray looks up from the turntables.

                    NICK

          Not to be nosey, but do you guys use protection?

                    SAM

I'm on the shot.

                    NICK

What about condoms?

                    SAM

No.

                    NICK

          He told us he was serious about catching something.

He cheated on you a lot, ya
know.

SAM

That motherfucker. If he
gave me something, I swear
I'll kill him myself.

RAS ORAY

Calm down, Samantha.
Everyt'ing irie. Everything
cool. Doug's just blowin'
wind...he don't mean it, dat
motha' ass.

AM

That pisses me off. You
know what sucks? Deep down,
I know I will always be his
girl. I fucking love him,
and this is how he treats
me. I don't know if it
makes me sick, or
something, but...Christ. I
can't fucking stand it.

NICK

Eric told me he brought
some tramp home the other
night. Last night he left
my house with that Janessa

116

girl.

> SAM

Janessa? That whore fucks
everyone. I can't believe
this…Janessa.

> NICK

It makes you wonder how
many times he's screwed
some bitch and then screwed
you without washing his
dick off.

> RAS ORAY

> Nick, not nice, mon.

Sam hops up off the couch
and grabs her key chain
with Daffy Duck dangling
from it off the coffee
table.

> SAM

Where is he today? Big
Burgers?

> NICK

Yeah, he's working tonight.
I wouldn't bother him at
work though.

ANTHONY S. BUONI

                    RAS ORAY

          Nothing you can do while
          he's workin'.

                    SAM

          Oh, yeah? I'm gonna give
          him a piece of my mind.

                    NICK

          He's not gonna want to hear
          it.

                    SAM

          I don't care what he wants
          to hear, I'm not putting up
          with this shit.

                    NICK

          I guess I can't stop you.

    Nick gets up and embraces Sam.

                    NICK

          I know you say that you
          love him and all, but why
          not leave his ass in the
          dirt? He keeps on treating
          you like shit, and you keep
          on taking him back. He does
          not deserve you, Sam. You

                    118

can do so much better.

> SAM

I know I can.

> NICK

I think if you look around, you might find someone that is going to treat you better. Someone that will respect you.

Sam frowns.

> SAM

Nick, I've told you before. You and I…we're just friends.

> NICK

Just friends…right. Yeah.

> SAM

I'll call you later. After I find that asshole.

> NICK

Don't do anything too stupid, OK?

                    SAM

          I just need to talk to him.
          I hope he's not really
          serious about this shit.
          I'll have to flog him to
          death if he is.

Nick chuckles.

                    RAS ORAY

          Don't get any trouble over
          him—he's not worth dat
          noise.

                    SAM

          Thanks, guys.

                    RAS ORAY

          Peace be wit you, peace be
          wit you.

INT. BIG BURGERS—EVENING

Doug, dressed in a BIG BURGER uniform,
stands behind the counter by one of
the three cash registers.

He hands change to a PRETTY FEMALE
CUSTOMER wearing too much makeup, a
short, red skirt, red pumps, and gaudy

hoop earrings with dolphins hanging
from them.

                    DOUG

          Eighty-six cents is your
          change, nice lady.

               PRETTY CUSTOMER

          Thank you, kind sir.

                    DOUG

          Please, call me Doug.

               PRETTY CUSTOMER

          OK, thanks, Doug.

                    DOUG

          Hey, are you a local? I
          don't recognize you.

               PRETTY CUSTOMER

          Well, I just moved here
          from Virginia.

                    DOUG

          Cool, I just know you're
          gonna love living here.
          That salt air gets in your
          blood.

Doug puts his elbows on the service
counter and leans in closer to her.

DOUG

Say, what's *your* name?

PRETTY CUSTOMER

My name is—

The front door to the restaurant flies
open and Sam barges in.

SAM

You no good, limp dick
motherfucker.

The pretty customer takes her food-
covered tray and retreats to a table
in the far corner.

DOUG

Hey, Sam, how's it going?

SAM

How many times did you
cheat on me—what if you
gave me something?

DOUG

Calm down, baby. It's all

good.

             SAM

It's not all good, asshole.

SANDRA, a woman in her late twenties dressed in a black manager shirt and black slacks, comes to the counter and crosses her arms.

             SANDRA

What's going on here, Doug?

             SAM

             (loud)

I'll tell you what's going on: Doug is trying to catch and spread STDs.

Doug chuckles.

             DOUG

That's crazy. Who would do such a thing?

             SAM

Son of a bitch, everybody's talking about it. I was the last one to know. What's with you and Janessa? Are

you fucking that dirty
skank?

            SANDRA

All right, I've had enough.
Doug, you're off. You need
to take your girl home and
get some things
straightened out.

            SAM

I'm not going anywhere with
him.

            SANDRA

Look, talk to Doug or don't
or whatever—just not here.
This is a business, not a
soap opera. Just leave.
I've had enough antics for
the day with the shake
machine crapping out and C-
shell and Layla calling the
cops on that freak.

            DOUG

All right, we're outta
here.

Doug walks over to the cash
register on the far right

and clocks out, tearing his
time slip from the
machine's printer.

                    DOUG

Will you at least give me a
ride home, Sam?

Sam thinks for a BEAT.

                    SAM

I'll give you a ride home,
but if you touch me—I'll
slap you so Goddamned hard…

                    SANDRA

That's enough. Take it
somewhere else, I don't
want to hear any more.

                    DOUG

Don't worry, we're going.

INT. SAM'S CAR—SUNSET

Doug and Sam are riding in Sam's
little, blue car as NEW WAVE music
softly plays.

                    SAM

Nineteen times? Was I not good enough for you?

DOUG

You were all right.

SAM

What do you mean by that?

DOUG

Occasionally you would get into it, but most of the time you would just lay there.

SAM

What?

DOUG

Besides, you would never let me do anything too kinky with you.

SAM

I'm afraid to ask, but like what?

DOUG

Let's see…

Doug thinks for a BEAT, scratching his chin.

                    DOUG

        I know for a fact you
        wouldn't let me donkey
        punch you.

                    SAM

        Donkey punch, what's that?

                    DOUG

        That's when I'm giving you
        anal, and I smack ya in the
        back of the head so you
        clamp up and feel tighter.

                    SAM

        I knew I should have never
        asked. Doug, I think you
        have a problem.

                    DOUG

        I got a lot of problems,
        what'cha gonna do?

                    SAM

Do you really? OK, so tell
me what your problems are.

DOUG

What?

SAM

I'm serious. I want to know
what's so damned wrong in
your life that you want to
go out and hunt down AIDS.

DOUG

Well, for starters, look at
me.

SAM

And?

DOUG

I'm wearing a fucking Big
Burger uniform. I'm twenty-
eight years old, and I work
in a fast food hell-hole.

SAM

That's easy to fix—get
another job.

DOUG

It's not that easy… The
worst part is that I'm used
to it. And another thing,
I'm gonna be dead by the
time I'm forty if I don't
stop boozing and drugging.

             SAM

Can you stop yourself, or
are you going to need
professional help?

             DOUG

That's just it—I don't want
help. I wasn't complaining
till you brought it up.
Everybody's gotta die
someday, somehow.

             SAM

You really don't care if
you catch something, do
you?

The car falls quiet for a BEAT. Doug
CRACKS HIS KNUCKLES as Sam stares
toward the road.

             SAM

Do you really mean all that shit, or is it just a sick joke?

DOUG

I mean it.

Sam slams on the brakes; we hear the TIRES SQUEAL.

DOUG

Sam, you can't stop here, we'll be hit.

SAM

I thought you've accepted that everybody dies.

DOUG

But—

SAM

Get out.

DOUG

Sam—

SAM

> I mean it. Get the fuck out
> now, Doug.

Doug sighs and opens the passenger
door, stepping out.

                    DOUG

> You can always call me when
> you want to have a little
> fun.

Sam speeds away, leaving Doug alone on
the empty road.

We hear LOUD HOUSE MUSIC and:

CUT TO:

INT. THE MOZZY—LATER THAT NIGHT

The Mozzy is crowded, and Doug,
wearing a yellow shirt and black
slacks fastened with a gold belt,
approaches DARREN, a guy in his early
thirties, conservatively dressed in
brown slacks and a blue button-up
shirt.

                    DOUG

> Darren. What up, playa?

They shake hands.

> DARREN

> Doug, how are you tonight?

> DOUG

> Could be better, I could
> have a date.

> DARREN

> You know I can help you
> with that. I know where
> there are *several* lovely
> ladies that are all alone
> tonight.

> DOUG

> Sounds intriguing. What
> would the damage be on
> that?

> DARREN

> For you, a friendly price.
> Ninety dollars, take it or
> leave it.

> DOUG

> Ninety bucks? Damn, you

pimps are killing me.

> DARREN

Gotta pay the bills, ya
know.

> DOUG

Ninety bucks…your girls
aren't as good-looking as
Griff's.

> DARREN

Griff? You're full of shit,
there's nothing wrong with
my girls.

> DOUG

Anyhow, I guess I'll try to
find a date the old-
fashioned way. If I strike
out, I'll let you hook me
up.

> DARREN

You know where to find me,
D-burger.

Doug walks across the dance floor and
notices Eric, wearing shiny, plastic
clothes.

ERIC

I thought I'd find you
here. Do you want to hit
Newby's afterwards?

DOUG

I want to find me a choice
piece of ass and ride that
shit all night long.

ERIC

You just don't stop, do
you?

DOUG

All go, no slow…besides, I
can't help it—I have a
twenty-four hour erection.
I need to wax some ass
fast.

ERIC

I hate to piss on your
raging libido, but Sam's
pretty pissed at you. That
girl loves you, man. That's
a rare thing. You shouldn't
walk away so easily. If
you're not careful, Nick is
gonna swoop in and snake

her from you.

DOUG

He can have her. They
deserve each other, those
fucking losers.

ERIC

Do you hear yourself?
You're outta control, cat.

DOUG

She's probably already
fucking that twat anyways.
I don't need either of
them. Man, fuck her.

ERIC

Man, *fuck you*. You're
hurting yourself. Janessa
told me you both shot coke
last night. What the fuck
are you doing? Get it
together, man. I'm not
gonna kick it with a
junkie. I'm also not going
to watch you throw you life
away so you can get all the
pussy you want.

DOUG

> Screw you. You're not the
> boss of me. I'll do what I
> want.

Doug turns and walks away from Eric to one the Mozzy's many bars and sits on a barstool, pulling out money.

DOUG

> Jagermeister, Ryan.

RYAN, a bartender in his early twenties, wearing a Mozzy shirt, pours Doug a shot of the black liquor.

RYAN

> How can you drink this
> crap?

Doug slams the shot.

DOUG

> Whew. That's the nectar of
> the gods, there. That shit
> raises the hairs in my
> asshole.

Ryan laughs.

DOUG

> Beer me, dog.

> RYAN

No prob.

Ryan slides a beer in front of Doug.

> RYAN
>
>> On me, dude. Thanks for
>> that, last week.

Doug nods.

> RYAN
>
>> Lots of girls here tonight.

> DOUG
>
>> I'm just wondering which
>> one's going home with me.

They laugh. Doug gets up and enters
the crowd of dancing people.

On the edge of the dance floor, Doug
notices a RAVER GIRL wearing a shirt
that says THE DAMNED, moving to the
rhythm of the intense music. He
approaches her like a hungry predator.

> DOUG
>
>> Hey, baby, wanna dance?

RAVER GIRL

Get lost, creep.

DOUG

Ouch—later, bitch.

He turns and almost bumps into WILLIE,
a man in his mid-twenties wearing a
tight, silver shirt and black slacks
with bright red flames up the sides. A
cigarette dangles in his right hand.

WILLIE

Your name's Doug, right?

DOUG

Umm, yeah, do I know you?

WILLIE

No, but we have a mutual
friend. You know that
little candy kid, Janessa?

DOUG

Oh, yeah.

WILLIE

Well, we drink sometimes.

Willie winks knowingly at Doug.

> WILLIE
>
> She had something really interesting to say about you.

> DOUG
>
> Oh yeah, what's that?

> WILLIE
>
> She told me you were bugchasing.

> DOUG
>
> What?

> WILLIE
>
> Bugchasing: trying to catch STDs. There are two kinds of cats, cat, the Giftgivers and the Bugchasers. Chasers are looking to become to HIV positive, or become Poz, for, you know, erotic thrill. With some, it is political, a protest towards the taboo of gay or alternative sex. Some

actually want to hurt other
people. Some do it to get a
free ride from the
government's Section 8
benefits.

DOUG

I've never heard of this.
And Giftgivers?

WILLIE

They're the ones with the
disease, though not always
the "high-five", if ya
catch my drift. They host
conversion parties where
Chasers can hook up and
gamble. Janessa told me you
were looking for one.

DOUG

She told you that?

WILLIE

Like I said, we're friends.

DOUG

I forgot. She knows
everybody.

       WILLIE

Anyways, my name's Willie
and I want to help you.

       DOUG

Do you know someone who's
looking for a date?

       WILLIE

Me, silly. Why don't *we*
spend the night together?
I've lived a lifetime of
casual sex and drug abuse.
If you're really
bugchasing, I'm a sure bet.

       DOUG

I'm sorry, Willie, but I'm
straight.

       WILLIE

Oh, don't be like that.
Hear me out, you like sex
right?

       DOUG

Who doesn't?

       WILLIE

And what is it about sex
that has you so enthralled?

DOUG

Everything. The kissing,
the heavy breathing, the
closeness…

WILLIE

We could have all that.

DOUG

I like pussy, Willie.

WILLIE

Look, handsome, fish is
overrated. If you are
really into sex, you gotta
try a non-breeder at least
once.

DOUG

I don't know…

WILLIE

Hey, you've had you've dick
sucked before, right?

DOUG

Sure, hundreds of times.

> WILLIE

Then you know what the problem is when a bitch gives head.

> DOUG

You've gotten head from a girl?

> WILLIE

Of course, and I've found that most of them don't know what the fuck they're doing.

> DOUG

Yeah, one will use too much teeth, and the next one won't use enough

> WILLIE

Most bitches won't even use their hands.

> DOUG

> (laughing)

Dumb sluts.

WILLIE

Look, I'm a guy, and I know
what guys like. I can suck
a mean cock, and since I
know you're a virgin, I'll
be real gentle.

DOUG

I still don't know, my
buddy's got these hookers…

WILLIE

Don't spend your money. How
'bout this? Why don't you
come to this little place I
know and have a couple of
drinks? We can see what
happens.

DOUG

Well—

WILLIE

I wont take no for an
answer. I have plenty of
party favors.

DOUG

Party favors? Like
what?

> WILLIE

Why don't you come and find
out?

Doug thinks a BEAT.

> DOUG

All right. You're intense,
man. I'm not promising
anything, but let's see
what happens.

Willie smiles and reaches into his
black, fire pants and pulls out a
clasped hand.

> WILLIE

Say *ahh*, starfighter.

Doug opens his mouth and Willie shoves
in a handful of blue pills. As he
chews, we see Doug's face turn sour.

> WILLIE

Just keep on chewing.
You'll thank me later.

Willie pops a couple of pills in his
mouths and chews them, expressionless.

                    DOUG

          I've never eaten any X
          that's tasted like that.

                    WILLIE

          Then you've been getting
          ripped off. Let's split,
          hotness.

EXT. CABIN IN THE WOODS—NIGHT

A lone cabin nestled deep in the
forest north of Bay County.

As Willie turns off his headlights, a
mysterious red light pours from the
cabin's windows.

INT. WILLIE'S CAR—NIGHT

Willie and Doug sit in the darkened
car in front of the cabin.

                    WILLIE

          Are you ready to party?

                    DOUG

          I'm fucked up, man. Where

are we? Is this where you live?

                    WILLIE

This isn't my house. This is where the vampires meet.

                    DOUG

Vampires?

                    WILLIE

The children of the night, what sweet music *we* make.

Willie opens his car door.

EXT. CABIN DOOR—CONTINUING

Doug and Willie stand side-by-side before the cabin door. Willie knocks three times and then two times. All is quiet for a BEAT.

                    DOUG

        What—

Willie puts his arm on Doug's shoulder as the cabin door slowly creeks open.

Standing in the doorway is a HOODED

MIDGET, wearing only leather pants, half the size of Doug and Willie.

                    HOODED MIDGET

          Who's the catch, Will?

                    WILLIE

          Grade A sexy, JP. We'll be
          having the usual tonight.

The hooded midget stares Doug up and down a BEAT and then steps out of the way. Willie leads Doug into the cabin.

INT. VAMPIRE LODGE—CONTINUING

The main room of the vampire lodge has several people of both sexes taking lines off a glass table in a darkened corner.

A bearded man flips over tarot cards, exposing more cocaine. Across from them, two guys are making out, pulling at each other's clothes.

                    WILLIE

          Don't mind them—here, take
          this.

Doug opens his mouth, and Willie

tosses him another pill.

>   WILLIE
>
>   That's some of the best LSD
>   this town has ever seen.
>   Hold on to your toenails,
>   because this candy-flip's
>   gonna blow you…

He leers at Doug, looking him up and
down, devouring him with his eyes.

>   WILLIE
>
>   …away.

The hooded midget opens a door leading
out of the main room. Willie ushers in
Doug.

INT. TORTURE ROOM—CONTINUING

The hooded midget flips on a BLUE
LIGHT, revealing WENDY, a naked woman
with red and black streaked hair,
drawn to an iron, four-post bed by
leather shackles. She smiles when she
sees them enter.

>   WILLIE
>
>   Doug, meet Wendy. She
>   doesn't talk much, but

>   she'll do anything you want
>   her to. Good morning,
>   Wendy.

                    WENDY

          What 'cha got for me?

Willie goes over to one side of the
iron bed and sits down next to Wendy,
pulling a handful of pills from his
pocket.

                    WILLIE

          How many?

                    WENDY

           All of them…all of them…

Willie laughs and feeds her.

The hooded midget produces a large
green bottle labeled ABSINTHE and
gives Wendy a sip to wash down the
pills; a green rivulet runs down her
cheek.

Willie hops off the bed as the hooded
midget pulls out an electronic tazer
from underneath the bed. Wendy giggles
with delight.

> WILLIE

Go ahead, give it to her.

The hooded midget zaps Wendy with the tazer and she squeals.

> HOODED MIDGET

Tomorrow, Wendy, you're going to die.

> WENDY

Again.

The hooded midget zaps her again; she sardonically laughs.

> WILLIE

Do you like her?

> DOUG

I've never seen anything like this before. Wow.

> WILLIE

You may have her…as I'm having you.

The midget zaps Wendy again.

                    WENDY

          Oh, God, hurt me. Fuck my
          pussy.

Willie leans in and kisses Doug as he
loosens his belt.

INT. DOUG'S BEDROOM—MORNING

Doug sleeps in his messy
bedroom.

A PHONE RINGS.

Doug answers a blue, corded
phone on his nearby, cluttered
nightstand, knocking over an
overflowing astray and a beer
bottle.

                    DOUG

          Hello? Oh, hey, Eric. Yeah,
          I've been laying low. No,
          I'm not mad. It's OK, we
          can talk about it later.
          Damn, you wouldn't believe
          the shit I saw a couple
          weeks ago. I know. I know.
          Was she really? I knew that
          Sam still wanted me. Ha,
          ha, ha. All right, tonight

> we'll hit Newby's and kick
> it. See ya.

Doug gets out of bed; he is wearing
boxers dotted with green, four-leaf
clovers. We follow him out of the
bedroom and into the bathroom where he
weighs himself.

Doug stands in front of the toilet and
with his back turned to us, he pulls
the front of his boxers down.

DOUG URINATES.

DOUG

> Oh, Jesus, fuck me,
> asshole—Goddamn.

Doug staggers.

His knees buckle.

He catches his balance on the back of
the toilet. After a BEAT, he
straightens himself out.

DOUG

> OK, come on, little guy. We
> can do this.

URINE TRICKLING.

DOUG

>   Ouch—fuck—mother, fuck me.

Doug turns around, tears streaming down his face.

INT. FREE CLINIC WAITING ROOM—LATER

Doug, wearing jeans and faded blue shirt with a turntable on it, sits in a plastic, blue chair in the waiting room and drums his fingers on the armrest. Outdated issues of junk magazines piled on a small table next to him.

A water fountain has an "out of order" sign dangling on it.

The only other person there is GERALD, a well-dressed fellow in his late twenties, who is reading an issue of *Golfer.*

As Doug drums harder on his armrest, Gerald looks up from his magazine, annoyed.

>   GERALD

>   That's annoying.

>   DOUG

Sorry, I'm sorry.

GERALD

It's OK. I can tell you're
nervous. Don't worry,
whatever happens, happens.

DOUG

Thanks. I've never done
this before. I didn't
realize how intense this
could be.

GERALD

Yeah, it's wild.

DOUG

Any good articles in there?

GERALD

Not really. Mostly crap
that has nothing to do with
my dull life.

DOUG

The only magazine I can
stomach is *Rolling Stone*. I
like reading Gregory
Freeman's articles.

GERALD

Rolling Stone is pretty good. A music fan, huh?

DOUG

I love all kinds.

GERALD

Me too. Hey are you from around here. I've lived here all my life, and I don't know who you are. That's weird, because you look about my age.

DOUG

Yeah, my name's Doug. I've lived here forever.

GERALD

Crazy, just when ya think you know everybody. The name's Gerald.

They shake hands.

DOUG

So, if you're a local, what kind of work do you do?

GERALD

I work the blood collection
van. We go around, place to
place, and collect the
blood that people donate.
Are you here for treatment?

DOUG

I'm here to be checked.

GERALD

Me too—the company likes to
screen because I'm working
with bodily fluids…it's
really no big whoop. You
get used to it after a
while. It becomes just
another part of the job.
Life goes on. Sometimes a
buzz is the only way to
shake things up, know what
I mean?

Doug nods.

DOUG

Christ, don't I.

GERALD

ANTHONY S. BUONI

Say, do you like imported
beers?

DOUG

Sure, I do.

GERALD

Then let's exchange
numbers. I know this little
local bar where you can get
the best imports and hang
out with cool people.

DOUG

Sure, but I think I need a
few days.

Gerald writes his number down on a
page of *Golfer* with a pen from his
pocket and tears the magazine to hand
Doug the information.

DOUG

Cool.

GERALD

May I have your number?

DOUG

Sure.

Doug grabs the pen and magazine from Gerald and writes his number on a different page, tearing it out, and handing it to Gerald.

GERALD

We'll party.

DOUG

Call me.

A NURSE, dressed in her uniform and holding a clipboard, opens the door across the waiting room.

NURSE

Doug Strobel?

Doug hops off his chair.

DOUG

That's me.

NURSE

Dr. Roney will see you now.

DOUG

Nice meeting you, Gerald.

GERALD

Good meeting you too, Doug.
Hey, I'm gonna call you,
OK?

DOUG

Sure, whenever you get the
time, we'll get wasted.

G   ERALD

Sounds like a party.

Doug nods and they shake hands again,
ending with a unison snap of their
fingers.

Doug follows the nurse into the back
of the building.

INT. DR. RONEY'S OFFICE—CONTINUING

Doug sits on white paper pulled over
an examination table in the center of
the office.

A waist-high cabinet filled with
medical supplies covers the left-hand
wall. Various anesthetic bottles,
plastic wrapped cotton swabs, plastic

wrapped syringes, and a box of tissue paper line the top of the cabinet.

On the back wall, there is a red box with the words "BIOHAZARD" above and below the pointed, circular symbol. Next to the box, several posters warn about the dangers of smoking and unsafe sex.

The door opens and DR. RONEY, a tall, well-built guy, wearing a white lab coat ENTERS. A stethoscope dangles around this neck. Dr. Roney flips through a clipboard of Doug's medical history.

                    DR. RONEY

          What seems to be the
          problem—

Dr. Roney looks at the first page of the clipboard.

                    DR.RONEY

          —Doug?

                    DOUG

          It hurts when I piss…it's
          like razorblades cutting
          the inside of my cock.

DR. RONEY

Do you practice safe sex?

DOUG

No.

Dr. Roney sighs.

DR. RONEY

There's all the reason in
the world to use
protection. Would you
consider yourself
promiscuous?

DOUG

A little.

DR. RONEY

Have you ever bought a
prostitute before?

DOUG

No.

DR. RONEY

Are you a drug user? Have
you ever shared needles?

DOUG

(softly)

Yes, I have.

DR. RONEY

Have you ever participated in same sex relations?

Doug is quiet a BEAT.

DR. RONEY

Doug, you are at high risk for numerous STDs. With the world being what it is, why would you live so hard, so fast?

DOUG

You don't wanna know.

DR. RONEY

Are you bugchasing, Doug?

Doug is quiet a BEAT.

DOUG

Yes.

Dr. Roney stares at Doug a BEAT.

DR. RONEY

Now, when you piss it
hurts. Look what you've
done to yourself. Are you
happy about this?

DOUG

No, sir.

DR. RONEY

It sounds to me that you've
either caught Chlamydia or
gonorrhea, but I won't know
until I take a Q-tip and
get a sample. That means
I'm gonna have to stick it
up your urethra. Does that
sound like fun, Doug?

DOUG

Not really, Doc.

DR. RONEY

There's a good chance that
you might also be stuck
with some disease that you
can't get rid of for the
rest of your life.

DOUG

I know.

DR. RONEY

All right, we'll run the
necessary tests and see
what we're dealing with.

DOUG

Cool.

DR. RONEY

Doug, I'm a single man. I
have women too. But I'm
safe, Doug, preventing
disease. You know what they
say about Bay County?

DOUG

No, what?

DR. RONEY

That you don't lose your
girlfriend, you just lose
your turn. You gotta keep
them and yourself clean so
when the right one comes
around, you can enjoy that
special thing. All joking
aside, in the future, I
want you to use these.

Dr. Roney opens the cabinet and puss out a small, brown paper bag. He tosses it to Doug, who catches it in midair.

Doug opens the bag and pulls out a handful of multicolored condoms. Doug smiles.

                    DOUG

          Thanks. This sucks, man. I
          promise I'll be more
          careful.

                    DR. RONEY

          I'm going to ask that you
          leave a list for the nurse
          of all the sexual partners
          you've had in the past year
          so we can call them to come
          get checked out. It will be
          anonymous, so you'll be
          spared embarrassment. Can
          you handle that?

                    DOUG

          Sure, no problem.

                    DR. RONEY

All right, are you ready to
get started?

DOUG

Let's do it.

CUT TO:

INT. JANESSA'S LIVING ROOM/KITCHEN—
THREE WEEKS LATER

Doug, dressed in sweat pants and a T-
shirt, is watching Janessa, wearing a
blue wife beater and a yellow skirt,
shoot up.

Janessa's candle, spoon, a syringe,
toothpick, and belt lie on the counter
beside her mirror that has a large
amount of cocaine on it.

JANESSA

This stuff isn't as good as
that shit we shot. Oh well,
you get what ya pay for.

DOUG

Tell me about it. Did it
come from that same kid?

JANESSA

No, I bought it from some
other guy. Did you wanna
bang a little with me
tonight?

DOUG

No, I haven't felt like
getting high lately. Fuck,
I don't even know how long
it's been since I've had a
drink.

JANESSA

What brings you here? If
not for drugs, did ya wanna
fool around?

DOUG

Actually, I need to talk to
you about that. A few weeks
ago, I went to the free
clinic because it hurt when
I pissed.

JANESSA

Oh—did you catch something?

DOUG

Yeah, but it wasn't what I

expected.

>   JANESSA

What did the doctor say?

>   DOUG

He told me I had gonorrhea.

>   JANESSA

Can they cure it?

>   DOUG

Fortunately, yes. I'm on oral antibiotics.

>   JANESSA

Fortunately? I thought you wanted to catch something.

>   DOUG

I didn't think—

Doug falls quiet for a BEAT. He pulls out a smoke from his silver cigarette case and holds it in his right hand.

>   DOUG

I guess I didn't think it through. When I had to pee that one morning, it hurt

so bad that I wanted to
die. I'd never felt
anything like it. The
experience wasn't-good.

Doug lights the cigarette with his
Zippo.

DOUG

The experience wasn't sexy
or hot at all. It was kind
of shitty.

Doug is quiet for a BEAT as he takes a
long drag off his cigarette.

JANESSA

Can I get one of those?

DOUG

Of course, darling.

Doug pulls out another
cigarette and passes it to
Janessa. He then gives her
a light from his Zippo.

DOUG

Dr. Roney asked for a list
of all my sexual partners
so they can inform them to
come and get tested. It was

> too embarrassing, so I
> split before I left the
> list. That's really why I'm
> here. I came to tell you
> that you might want to go
> and get tested.

Janessa starts chopping her cocaine
with a black credit card.

> JANESSA
>
> I don't think I'm gonna do
> that, Doug.

> DOUG
>
> I thought you said you were
> being silly not going and
> getting checked out.

Janessa puts some powder onto her
carbon-burned spoon.

> JANESSA
>
> I just don't care. So what
> if I do catch something?
> Fuck it if I hurt. I
> already hurt, but the pain
> gets washed away every
> night

Janessa uses her eyedropper and
squeezes a couple of drops of water

onto the spoon.

> JANESSA
>
> Everybody's gotta die—
> right?

Janessa begins stirring the concoction with a toothpick.

> DOUG
>
> I guess there's nothing I
> can say. Will you do me a
> favor?

> JANESSA
>
> Sure, anything, doll face.

Janessa puts the spoon over the lit candle.

> DOUG
>
> Will you let Willie know
> that he needs to be tested?
> I'm not sure how to find
> him.

> JANESSA
>
> No problem, sweetie. Are
> you sure you don't want a
> hit?

DOUG

Nah, I've got a couple of
people I've got to talk to.

JANESSA

Aw, come on, Doug. Look,
you don't have to shoot
any, just rip a rail with
me. Okay, you caught me. I
have some better shit. I
was saving it, but since
you're so sexy…

Doug watches as she pulls out several
bagged eight balls from a wooden box
beside her. She empties one on the
mirror and chops at it with the credit
card.

JANESSA

I got some on front from
this cat, Hunter.

DOUG

You shouldn't out the
pusher, girl. That's bad
form.

JANESSA

>   Oh, hush. Who are you
>   telling? Anyways, I've been
>   showing him a good time,
>   and he's practically giving
>   this shit to me.

She sets up the coke in thick lines.

                    DOUG

>   Fuck, those aren't lines,
>   those are train tracks.
>   That's a lot of coke. If
>   you get caught…

                    JANESSA

>   Don't think like that. Now
>   is the part when you say
>   'thanks, Janessa, for
>   turning me on', and we
>   party.

Doug swallows hard. Janessa hands him a rolled up twenty.

                    JANESSA

>   After you, starfighter.

Doug takes a deep breath, places the end of the bill to his nostril, and snorts a line.

                    DOUG

> Damn, girl, that is fire.

JANESSA

> Take another.

Doug obeys, snorting more of the drug.

DOUG

> Fuck an A, I hate to drug
> and dash, but I got some
> shit I have to do.

He wipes some of the coke off the
mirror with his pointer finger,
sticking it in his mouth.

JANESSA

> I can tell you're on now. I
> know when I get started, it
> takes a handful of sleeping
> pills to get me to stop.
> Here, take one of these.

She hands him one of the eight balls.

DOUG

> I really don't need that.

JANESSA

Look, pay me whatever
whenever. I told you, he is
giving it to me really
cheap. I think we could
both get this moving and
make some money.

DOUG

Maybe.

JANESSA

Don't be shy, sexy. This is
business.

DOUG

I know, I'm just trying to
do things a little better.
Live right, ya know?

JANESSA

Pfft. How do you know this
isn't the way to live? It's
all perception.

DOUG

I suppose.

JANESSA

Just relax. Have fun. This
will pass. You're just
fucked up because of
everything that happened.
It's a little white fence,
and you'll be over it soon.

DOUG

I guess. Fuck, my nose is
running. I'd better get
trucking before my cock
gets hard.

JANESSA

You say it like it's a bad
thing. Whatever. Cool. Come
back later.

DOUG

I might.

Doug blows Janessa a kiss
as she tears apart a cotton
ball.

DOUG

Later, baby.

Janessa nods as Doug walks over to the
door, placing his hand on the
doorknob.

                    DOUG

              Janessa?

Janessa looks up and we see that the
syringe is now in her arm.

                    DOUG

              Take care of yourself,
              Okay?

                  JANESSA

              Sure thing, baby.

Doug opens the door and EXITS.

EXT. SHELIA'S HOUSE—LATE AFTERNOON

Doug, occasionally sniffing, is
standing in front of a closed door. He
sighs and raises his hank to knock,
but pauses a BEAT. Then he knocks
three times and then two times and
waits another BEAT.

Shelia, wearing jeans and a white
button-up shirt tied in a knot on the
front, opens the door. Upon realizing
who is standing in front of her, she
crosses her arms.

                  SHELIA

I told you if I saw you
around here, I would call
the fucking cops. Why the
fuck are you here, Doug?

DOUG

Shelia, I'm sorry to bother
you. I know I'm not a
person that you want to
see.

SHELIA

That's the understatement
of the fucking century.

DOUG

Anyhow, I have to apologize
because I—

Doug hesitates for a BEAT.

SHELIA

Spit it out.

DOUG

Somewhere I contracted
gonorrhea and, maybe, you
might want to go to the
free clinic and get tested.

Shelia's face goes from a look of

impatience to a glare of anger. She begins slapping and hitting Doug.

> SHELIA
>
> You fucking no good whore. You goddamn slut—you filthy piece of shit.

Doug backs up, blocking her assault with his arms.

> DOUG
>
> Shelia, stop…hey.

> SHELIA
>
> I told you I'd kill you if I got fucking sick.

> DOUG
>
> Hey, you might not be sick. You need to get checked, that's all. I'm so fucking sorry—

> SHELIA
>
> You asshole. You fuck me when I'm high, brag about trying to catch a disease, and now you come to my mother fucking house apologizing because *you* got

something. Look at you,
you're fucking high now.
You're a fucking loser,
Doug.

                    DOUG

Shelia—

                    SHELIA

Fuck you, Doug. I don't
ever want to see you again,
and I mean it. You come by
again, and you'll spend the
night in jail, you dead
fuck.

Shelia turns and storms back into her
house, slamming the door behind her.

Doug, sniffs, turns, and walks home.

                    DOUG

          Mission failed.

INT. DOUG'S HOUSE—EARLY EVENING

Sam and Doug are sitting on Doug's
green leather couch. The picture of
Bob Dylan is still resting on the
floor where it fell. The TV is tuned
to a VH1 Classic NEW WAVE marathon.

Doug, smoking a cigarette, is wearing a *PULP FICTION* T-shirt and torn blue jeans while Sam is wearing black slacks and a shirt with Robert Smith holding a guitar.

                    SAM

          I warned you—you didn't
          listen. Now look.

                    DOUG

          Yeah, it fucking sucks.

                    SAM

          Doug, I'm going to get
          tested tomorrow, and if I
          have something, I'll deal
          with it. I'm not angry with
          you—I'm beyond all that.
          Really, what's left is old-
          fashioned disappointment.

                    DOUG

          I'm sorry, Sam.

                    SAM

          Don't be sorry, Doug. What
          I want to hear from you is
          how you see yourself.
          You're obviously still

using. Are you still
bugchasing?

Doug is quiet a BEAT as he puts his
cigarette out in a blue seashell
shaped ashtray.

> DOUG
>
> When I first told you that,
> we were fighting and I was
> angry. I really didn't mean
> it. Then, I thought about
> it and it made a weird,
> twisted sense. I talked
> myself into believing it
> was what I wanted.

> SAM
>
> Then you caught something.

> DOUG
>
> You know, I had some good
> times—some wild
> experiences. They weren't
> worth the pain, though. The
> pain cheapened everything.

> SAM
>
> You didn't answer my
> question, Doug. Do you
> still want HIV?

DOUG

No, I'm through with that.

SAM

I'm still here for you. I'm still in love with you. I want to try and work things out. If you want to settle down—

DOUG

Sam, stop. You're a beautiful person. You're pretty, smart, and you have a heart of gold. I don't think I need to be in a relationship right now. After everything I've been through this past month, I feel…dirty. You still seem so pure—so clean. I don't want to taint you with my bullshit, Sam.

SAM

Doug, I—

DOUG

Listen, you can so much better. One day you're going to meet a guy who will treat you right, the way you deserve to be treated.

Sam's eyes fill with tears. She hops off the leather couch.

                    SAM

I need to get out of here. I got…laundry to do.

                    DOUG

All right.

Doug stands up and gives Sam a hug.

                    DOUG

See you later, okay?

                    SAM

Yeah, sure. Why do you have to be so goddamn stupid, Doug?

Doug chuckles and their embrace is broken.

                    DOUG

> I'll call you in a couple
> of days.

                    SAM

You do that.

Sam opens the front door but pauses a
BEAT. She points to the fallen Bob
Dylan poster.

                    SAM

> You should hang him back
> up.

                    DOUG

> Yeah.

Sam EXITS, gently pushing the door
shut behind her.

Doug pulls out his silver cigarette
case and removes a cigarette. Using
his Zippo, he lights up.

Doug walks over to the Bob Dylan
poster and hangs it back on the wall,
next to the door.

                    DOUG

> Sorry, Bobby. I didn't mean
> to neglect you.

A PHONE RINGS.

Doug walks into the kitchen where his phone rests on the counter. Doug picks up the black, cordless phone.

                    DOUG

          Hello? Oh, hey, Gerald.
          What's up? No, I don't have
          any plans. Where are you
          hanging out tonight? Beach
          Package? Oh, yeah, next to
          Sergeant Pepper's on the
          strip. Can ya pick me up?
          Cool, man…later, daddy-o.

INT. DOUG'S HOUSE—LATER

Doug snorts a line off a book and pinches his nostrils. He unfurls the rolled up hundred dollar bill he used as a straw, tucking it in his pocket. There is KNOCKING at the door and he wipes the residue off the book and licks it as he heads to answer it.

He opens the door, and Gerald, wearing tan cargo pants and a red Hawaiian shirt with white flowers, stands in the doorway.

                    GERALD

Evening, man. What's up?

DOUG

Come in. I'm almost ready.

Gerald ENTERS.

GERALD

Nice place. You renting or
owning?

DOUG

(sniffing)

Renting. I got a lame job
in Panama Shitty Beach,
Florida. There's no hope of
me coming up here.

GERALD

I hear a lot of people
blaming this place for
their woes. I think there's
more to it than that.

DOUG

I don't know, man. Seems
like the same thing day in
and day out.

GERALD

And you think things would
be different living
somewhere else?

DOUG

I don't know. Anyway, what
am I missing here?

Snot begins running from Doug's nose,
and he tries to wipe it away with his
arm. He is fidgeting, pacing around
the room looking for something he is
not sure he needs in the first place.

GERALD

Jesus, you're high as a
fucking angel fart, man.
What are you on? Coke?
Meth?

DOUG

Dude, I'm cool.

Gerald crosses his arms.

GERALD

Bullshit. For real, what
did you take? Some pills?

Doug offers nothing. He stares at

Gerald, jacking his lower jaw.

                    GERALD

          Look, man, I'm no cop. I
          party, too. If you want to
          get geeked, we can skip the
          bar and party here.

                    DOUG

          I'm not tweeking. I took a
          little blow.

                    GERALD

          Hell yeah. Want to match
          me?

                    DOUG

          Match you?

Gerald reaches in one of his pockets
and pulls out an oval carrying case.
He unzips it and we see several
syringes and a gram of cocaine.

                    GERALD

          Got a spoon?

                    DOUG

          Yeah, but I'll snort mine.

GERALD

No problem, but you're
wasting it.

Doug laughs as he pulls out his stash.
The two men dump their drugs out on
the same book Doug was using earlier.
Gerald begins chopping up the cocaine
with his driver's license as Doug
fetches a spoon from the kitchen.

When he returns, Gerald has lit a
candle on the counter and is rolling
up a hundred dollar bill. Despite
several lines covering the book, a
large pile of coke remains.

Doug hands him the spoon, and Gerald
begins the ritual.

GERALD

Got any booze?

DOUG

Vodka OK?

GERALD

Sure, I can sip that. Any
beer to wash it down?

DOUG

Just cheap shit.

GERALD

Perfect.

Doug retrieves two beers from the refrigerator and a bottle of vodka from a cabinet. He fills two shot glasses as Gerald shoots up.

DOUG

Here. Salud.

GERALD

Thanks. Na zdravie.

They clink glasses before knocking back the shot.

INT. DOUG'S HOUSE—CONTINUING

The candle has burned down. Several empty beer cans line the counter where Doug and Gerald sit, furthering their debauchery. The vodka, almost empty looms nearby.

DOUG

(sniffing and talking fast)

I really love her. I'm just
so fucked up, man.

            GERALD

Nah. You're not fucked up,
the world is. You just
happen to be living in it.

            DOUG

I don't know. Ya know, I
can fly straight. I can
change the way I am living
my life for her. I just
want her to work with me.

            GERALD

And then you both just ride
into the sunset, right?
Live happily ever after?

            DOUG

I know that's not how
things work for real. I
just… I just… Fuck, man.

He picks up the rolled hundred and
looks at the next line a BEAT.

            DOUG

Man, my connection was
right. Once you get started

on this shit, it's hard to
stop.

             GERALD

I got some pills if you
want. They'll put you down
in a bit.

             DOUG

Thanks. I'll probably need
them.

He places the bill in his nostril and
leans down to take the next rail.

             DOUG

FUCK.

             GERALD

What's wrong?

             DOUG

I can't fucking breathe
anymore. My fucking nose is
swollen shut.

Gerald laughs.

             GERALD

> Here, use one of these. I
> know you're no virgin.

He offers Doug a needle.

DOUG

> No, I really don't want to.

He tries to use the straw method
again. He SNORTS HARD, but has no
success,

DOUG

> FUCK, man.

Gerald shakes his head and loads a
syringe.

GERALD

> Give me your arm. This will
> make everything better.

Doug wipes his nose and offers his
arm. Gerald hands him a tourniquet.
After tightening it, Gerald finds a
vein and gives him a hit.

DOUG

> Shit, that's good.

Gerald smiles.

INT—DOUG'S HOUSE—CONTINUING

The candle has burned out; there is no
more cocaine left in the pile.

GERALD

Damn it, man. I have to
work in a few hours.

DOUG

I don't want to ever work
again.

GERALD

Ah, the American Dream. Go
on welfare. Seems to work
for a lot of those assholes
out there.

DOUG

I don't want to live like
that.

GERALD

Hoe do you want to live,
Doug?

Doug smiles.

> DOUG
>
> I don't know, man. You got those pills. I might try to crash, go talk to Sam later.

> GERALD
>
> You are a glutton for punishment. But if that's what you want…

Gerald gives him a few blue pills.

> GERALD
>
> Take care, dude. I'll be in touch. I had a blast. We'll have to do this again sometime. DOUG
>
> I don't think so. I really want to change my life. I can't keep this shit up.

> GERALD
>
> Sure, that's what they all say. Take care, kid.

Gerald EXITS as Doug swallows the pills, chasing them with beer.

INT. DOUG'S BEDROOM—EVENING

Doug's ringing cell wakes him up. He rolls over in his tangled sheets and answers.

                    DOUG

          Yo. Hey, Ras. Yeah. I'm
          good for a run. Wait…what
          time is it? Really?
          Wait…what **day** is it? Fuck,
          I've been out for two days.
          Dancing with the white
          devil, man. I know, I know.
          Can I do it tomorrow? I
          need to clean up and call
          Sam. Yeah. I know. I know.
          Thanks, man. Ciao.

He hangs up and looks at his arm, bruises run from his track marks. He shakes his head.

INT. DOUG'S HOUSE—LATER

Carrying a black plastic garbage bag, Doug picks up empty cans and other refuse scattered about his apartment. He comes across a picture of him and Sam, holding each other at a concert.

Running his hands over the image, his eyes swell with tears.

Doug puts down the photo, wipes his eyes, and pulls out his cell phone, scrolling through his contacts and calling Sam.

> DOUG
>
> Hey, Sam, it's me. Can we talk?

INT. SAM'S HOUSE—LATER

Sam answers the door, letting Doug ENTER. They exchange an awkward hug.

> DOUG
>
> I have a lot I want to say to you.

> SAM
>
> Yeah, well, I have a lot to say to you, too.

> DOUG
>
> Sam, I—

SAM

Cut the crap. You're still fucking using. I see your arm. Ya know, you tell me you can't be with me, you tell me you want to get straight—you tell me all sorts of things, Doug. But the sad thing is that it is not about me not knowing what I want, it's that you have no fucking idea what YOU want. I am too old for this roller coaster ride. As much as I care—no—love you, I have more respect for myself.

DOUG

You know I love you, Sam.

SAM

That doesn't matter anymore, Doug. I know how fucked up this world is. It's not just me and you, it's everyone.

DOUG

This world can be

beautiful, if you let it.

SAM

Only in dreams, Doug. But
we are not in a dream. We
are not in some fairy tale.
This is real life. This is
my life. And I'm, not gonna
waste another minute of it.

DOUG

So that's it?

Sam swallows hard.

SAM

That's it. I need time.
Right now is not good for
us…even as friends.

DOUG

Fuck.

SAM

When you said you were
trying to catch something,
I thought it was something
so depraved, that only you
could think of such a

thing.

                DOUG

No, it's not just me.

                SAM

Yeah. This guy got arrested
here yesterday—he was
tainting blood, trying to
spread HIV to everyone he
came across.

                DOUG

A giftgiver. Here?

                SAM

Yeah. A real sick-o too. He
worked for some blood
center. He was infecting
the donations. Can you
believe it?

                DOUG

Wait…what was this guy's
name?

                SAM

Oh…Gerald something. I
can't remember. I can't
believe you haven't heard.

> It's been all over the
> news. I know you don't
> watch much TV, but I
> thought it might have
> gotten through the
> whispers.

Doug looks at his bruised arm.

>   DOUG

> I think I know him… Fuck.

INT. DR RONEY'S OFFICE—FOUR MONTHS
LATER

Doug, wearing a gray sweat suit, and
Sam, wearing a navy blue shirt and
black jeans, are sitting on the
examination table in the center of Dr.
Roney's office.

>   SAM

> Don't worry, Doug, it'll be
> OK.

>   DOUG

> I'm scared, Sam. This is
> the rest of my fucking life
> we're talking about.

>   SAM

I know, honey.

Dr. Roney ENTERS, this time with two
clipboards in his hands.

DR. RONEY

I have your results, Doug.

SAM

Is he gonna be all right?

DR. RONEY

Doug, I'm sorry, but you're
HIV positive.

SAM

No!

DOUG

Fuck.

DR. RONEY

Are you two sleeping
together?

DOUG

No, I haven't had sex with
anyone.

                    DR. RONEY

          That's reassuring, but
          we're gonna have to retest
          you, too, Sam. Just to be
          safe.

                    SAM

          I don't mind.

                    DR. RONEY

          That guy is gonna fry for
          poisoning all that blood.

                    DOUG

          I hope he burns in hell.

Dr. Roney pulls out an oral HIV test
and unwraps it, handing it to Sam. We
see her put it into her mouth.

                    DR. RONEY

          Don't talk, now, it'll just
          take a moment.

The room falls quiet for a couple of
BEATS.

                    DR. RONEY

> That's long enough. I'm
> going to get this sent off,
> so, you two hang tight.

We see Dr. Roney slide the test into a plastic bag and write on it. He then exits the office.

> SAM

> Even if I'm negative, I
> still want to be with you,
> Doug.

> DOUG

> I love you, Sam. I could
> never hurt you.

> SAM

> I'll do anything for you.

> DOUG

> We can't be together
> anymore. I'm so fucking
> sorry, Sam. I'm so fucking
> sorry.

Tears swell up in Doug's eyes and stream down his face. He brushes them aside with his hands.

> SAM

CONVERSION PARTY

What are we going to
fucking do now?

DOUG

I honestly don't know…

FADE OUT

.

ABOUT THE AUTHOR

Living and creating in New Orleans, Louisiana, Anthony S. Buoni haunts swamps and bayous along the Gulf of Mexico, writing, editing, producing, and lecturing about his craft. He's co-edited and co-produced two exciting anthologies: *Distorted* and *Underwater*. Currently writing a New Orleans monster novel, he's also putting the final edits on novels featuring ghosts, zombies, and a café between life and death filled with secrets and philosophy. His next books, a collection of dark short stories and a somber zombie tale, are due for publication sometime in 2017. When not writing, Anthony is a Bourbon Street bartender, underground musician, and DJ, drawing down the moon with new wave, trance, and melancholy tunes. Other interests include film, gardening, comic books, and playing music and video games with his son, Fallon.

Visit his blog at nolashadowcat.com and explore working drafts of stories and novels as well as articles and essays about horror culture, music, writing, New Orleans, drinking, and travel.

JOIN THE TRANSMUNDANE COMMUNITY

🦋 Find your next favorite read.

🧍 Meet new authors to love.

⛺ Win free books and prizes.

🏹 Play games and join the community contests.

🤸 Watch the latest videos.

🐺 Share the infographics, memes, quizzes, and more!

www.transmundanepress.com
transmundanepress@gmail.com

Lightning Source UK Ltd.
Milton Keynes UK
UKHW050213141218
333977UK00028B/443/P